Hubble the cat
- Goal is world domination
- Loves tuna and tummy rubs
- Thinks he's smarter than humans

Marina Mon
- Super athlet
- Future Martian
- Doesn't get jokes

- Future career? Not sure.
- Can't fold laundry

WITHDRAWN

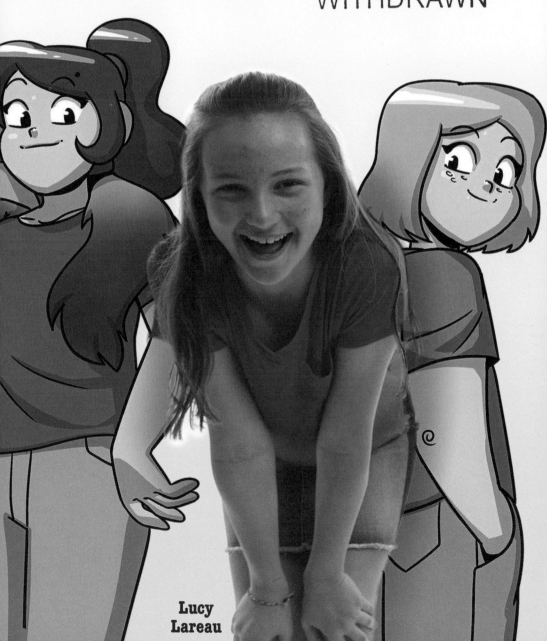

Lucy
Lareau

geeky f@b 5 ™

Lucy

Zara

Marina

A.J.

Sofia

Hubble

PAPERCUTZ

MORE GREAT GRAPHIC NOVEL SERIES AVAILABLE FROM PAPERCUTZ™

THE SMURFS #21

THE GARFIELD SHOW #6

BARBIE #1

THE SISTERS #1

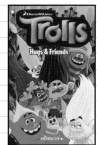
TROLLS #1

GERONIMO STILTON #17

THEA STILTON #6

SEA CREATURES #1

DINOSAUR EXPLORERS #1

SCARLETT

ANNE OF GREEN BAGELS #1

DRACULA MARRIES FRANKENSTEIN!

THE RED SHOES

THE LITTLE MERMAID

FUZZY BASEBALL

HOTEL TRANSYLVANIA #1

THE LOUD HOUSE #1

MANOSAURS #1

THE ONLY LIVING BOY #5

GUMBY #1

see more at papercutz.com
Also available wherever ebooks are sold.

geeky f@b 5 ™

#2 "Mystery of the Missing Monarchs"

LUCY & LIZ LAREAU — Writers
RYAN JAMPOLE & JEN HERNANDEZ — Artists

PAPERCUT Z ™
NEW YORK

geeky f@b 5™

#2 "Mystery of the Missing Monarchs"

LUCY & LIZ LAREAU–Writers
RYAN JAMPOLE–Layouts
JEN HERNANDEZ—Finished Art, pages 15-36
RYAN JAMPOLE—Finished Art, pages 5-14, 37-53
MATT HERMS—Colorist, pages 5-29
LAURIE E. SMITH—Colorist, pages 30-54
WILSON RAMOS JR.—Letterer
MANOSAUR MARTIN—Production
JEFF WHITMAN–Managing Editor
JIM SALICRUP
Editor-in-Chief

papercutz.com
geekyfabfive.com

ISBN: 978-1-5458-0156-7

Printed in India
March 2019

Papercutz books may be purchased for business or promotional use.
For information on bulk purchases, please contact Macmillan Corporate and Premium Sales Department at (800) 221-7945 x5442.

Distributed by Macmillan
First Printing

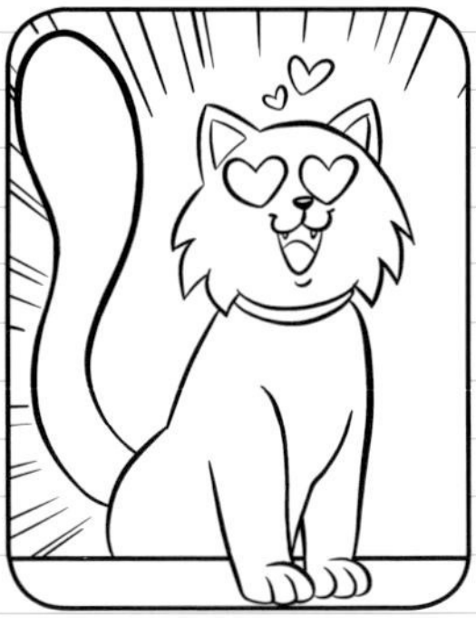

Teacher's Guide available at:
http://papercutz.com/educator-resources-papercutz

CHAPTER ONE: FOLLOW THE BOUNCING BALL...

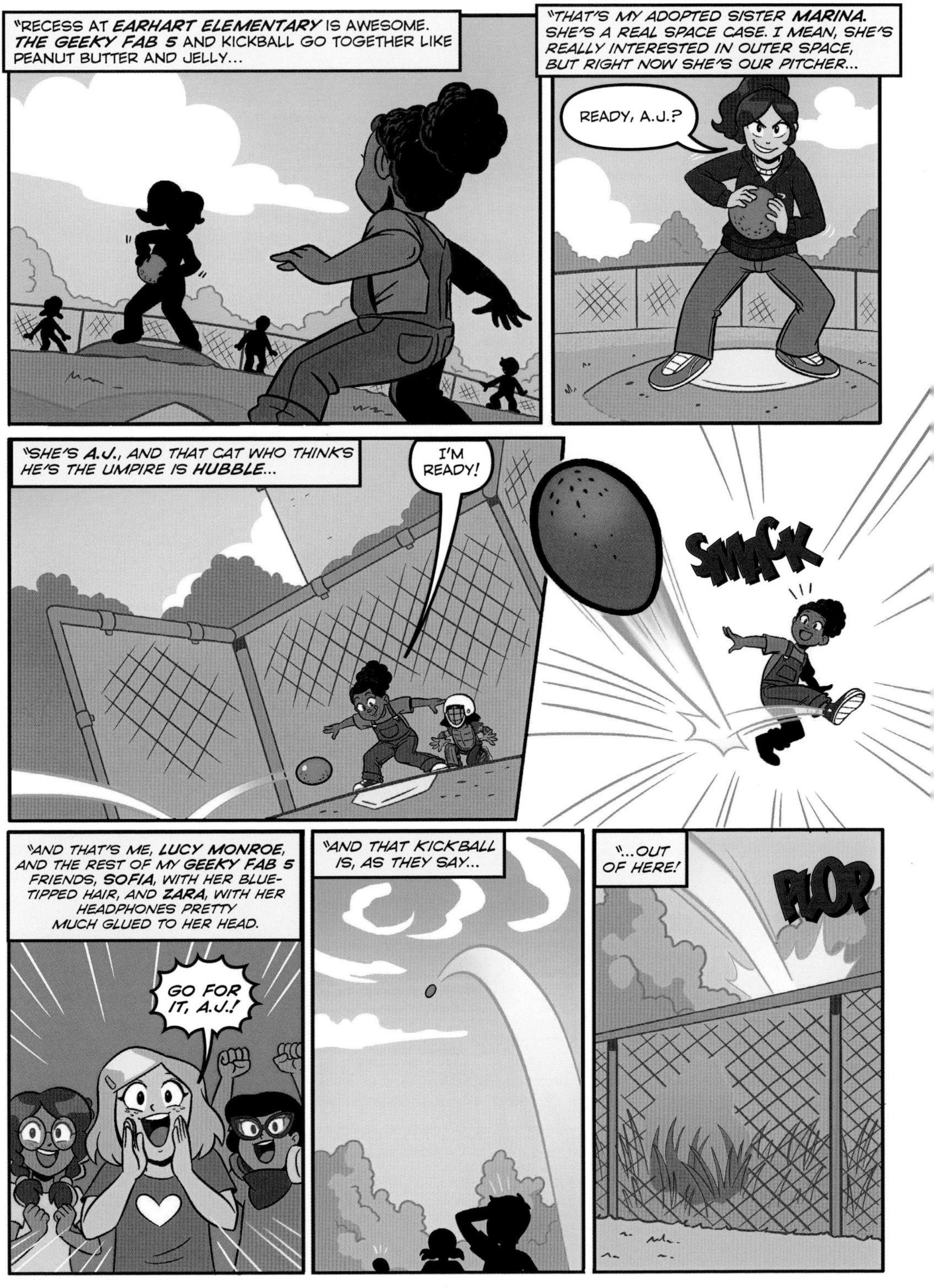
"RECESS AT EARHART ELEMENTARY IS AWESOME. THE GEEKY FAB 5 AND KICKBALL GO TOGETHER LIKE PEANUT BUTTER AND JELLY...
"THAT'S MY ADOPTED SISTER MARINA. SHE'S A REAL SPACE CASE. I MEAN, SHE'S REALLY INTERESTED IN OUTER SPACE, BUT RIGHT NOW SHE'S OUR PITCHER...
READY, A.J.?
"SHE'S A.J., AND THAT CAT WHO THINKS HE'S THE UMPIRE IS HUBBLE...
I'M READY!
SMACK
"AND THAT'S ME, LUCY MONROE, AND THE REST OF MY GEEKY FAB 5 FRIENDS, SOFIA, WITH HER BLUE-TIPPED HAIR, AND ZARA, WITH HER HEADPHONES PRETTY MUCH GLUED TO HER HEAD.
GO FOR IT, A.J.!
"AND THAT KICKBALL IS, AS THEY SAY...
"...OUT OF HERE!
PLOP

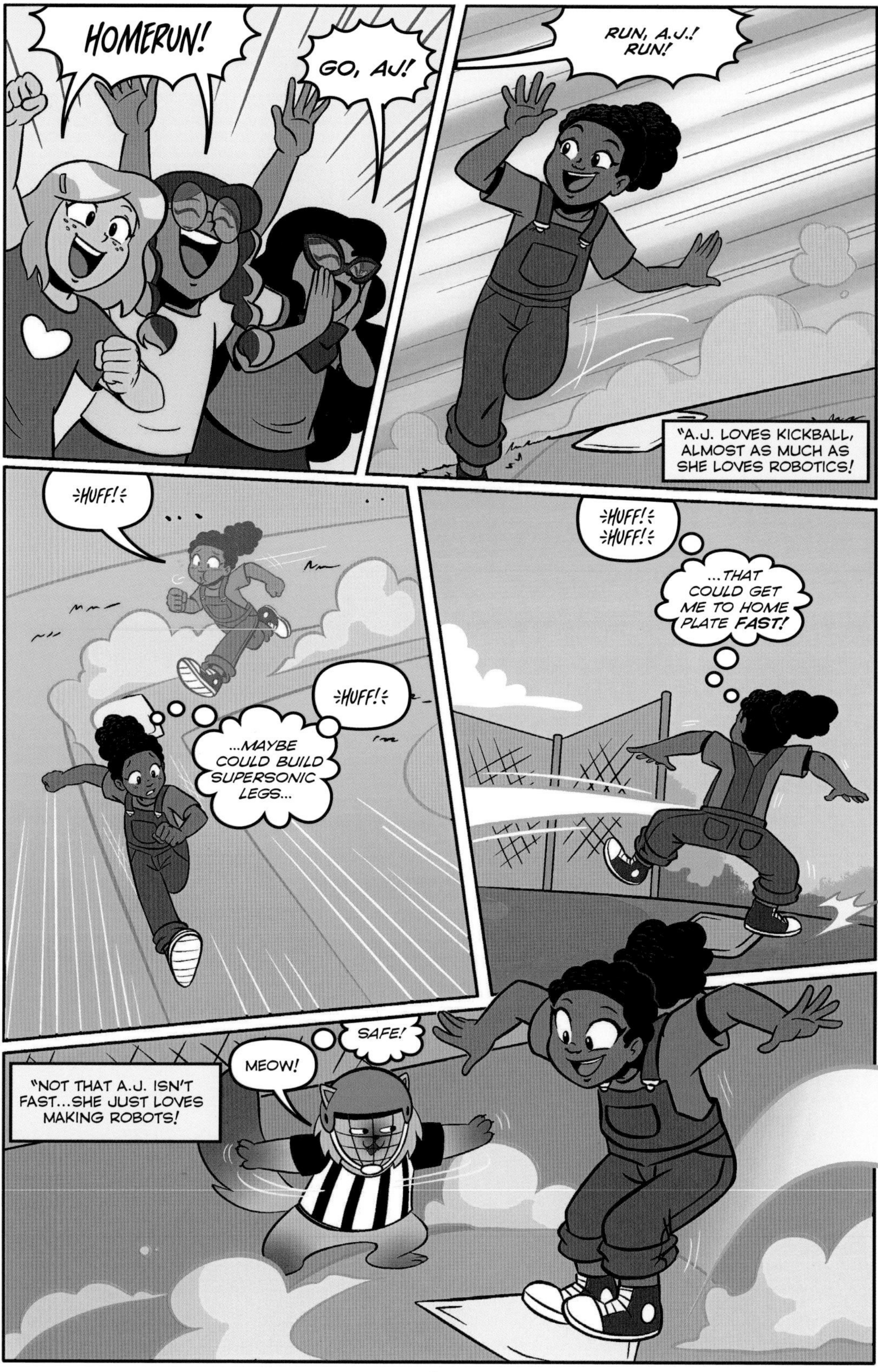
HOMERUN!
GO, AJ!
RUN, A.J.! RUN!
"A.J. LOVES KICKBALL, ALMOST AS MUCH AS SHE LOVES ROBOTICS!
HUFF!
HUFF!
...MAYBE COULD BUILD SUPERSONIC LEGS...
HUFF! HUFF!
...THAT COULD GET ME TO HOME PLATE FAST!
"NOT THAT A.J. ISN'T FAST...SHE JUST LOVES MAKING ROBOTS!
MEOW!
SAFE!

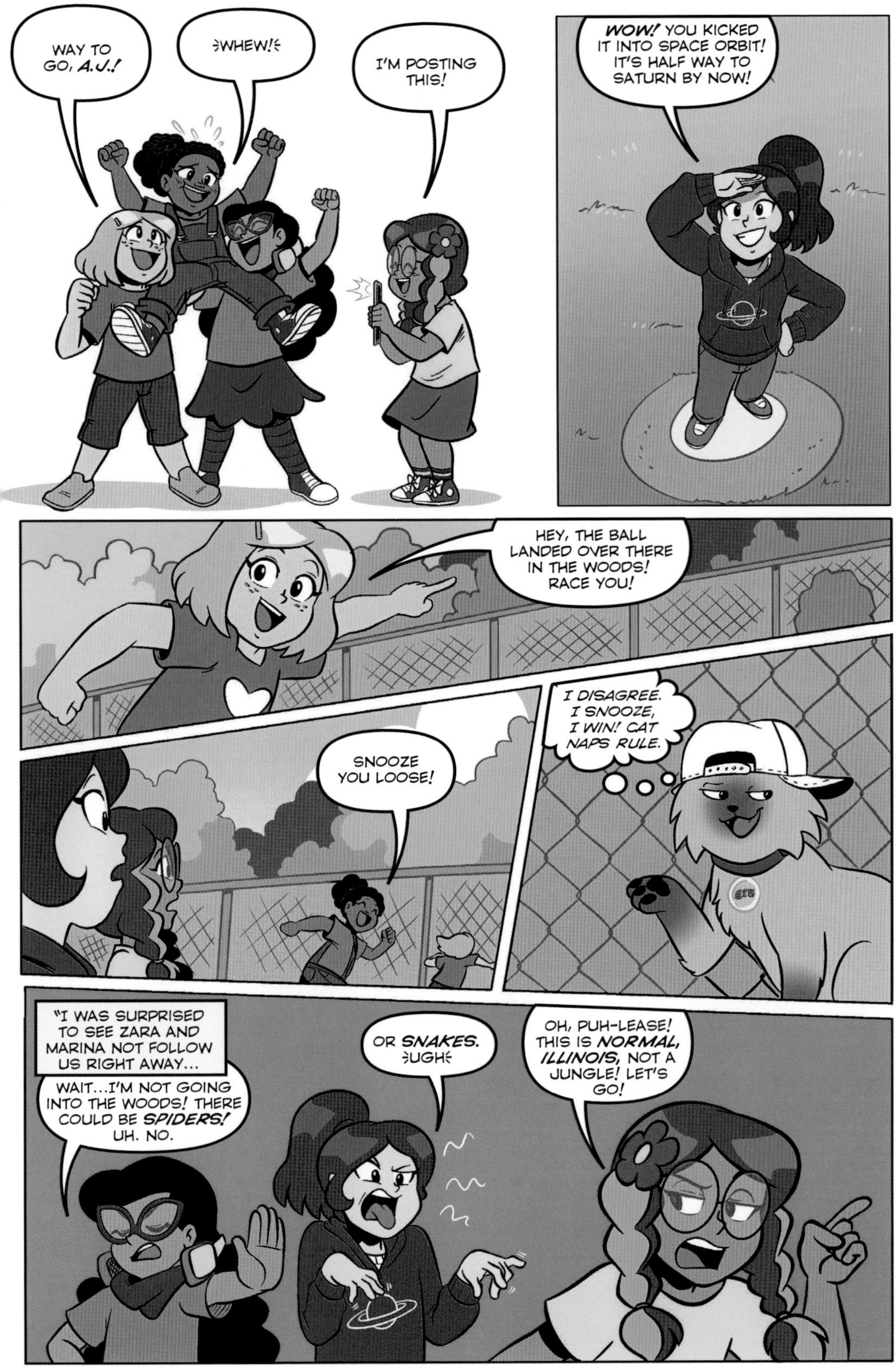
WAY TO GO, A.J.!
WHEW!
I'M POSTING THIS!
WOW! YOU KICKED IT INTO SPACE ORBIT! IT'S HALF WAY TO SATURN BY NOW!
HEY, THE BALL LANDED OVER THERE IN THE WOODS! RACE YOU!
SNOOZE YOU LOOSE!
I DISAGREE. I SNOOZE, I WIN! CAT NAPS RULE.
"I WAS SURPRISED TO SEE ZARA AND MARINA NOT FOLLOW US RIGHT AWAY...
WAIT...I'M NOT GOING INTO THE WOODS! THERE COULD BE SPIDERS! UH. NO.
OR SNAKES. UGH
OH, PUH-LEASE! THIS IS NORMAL, ILLINOIS, NOT A JUNGLE! LET'S GO!

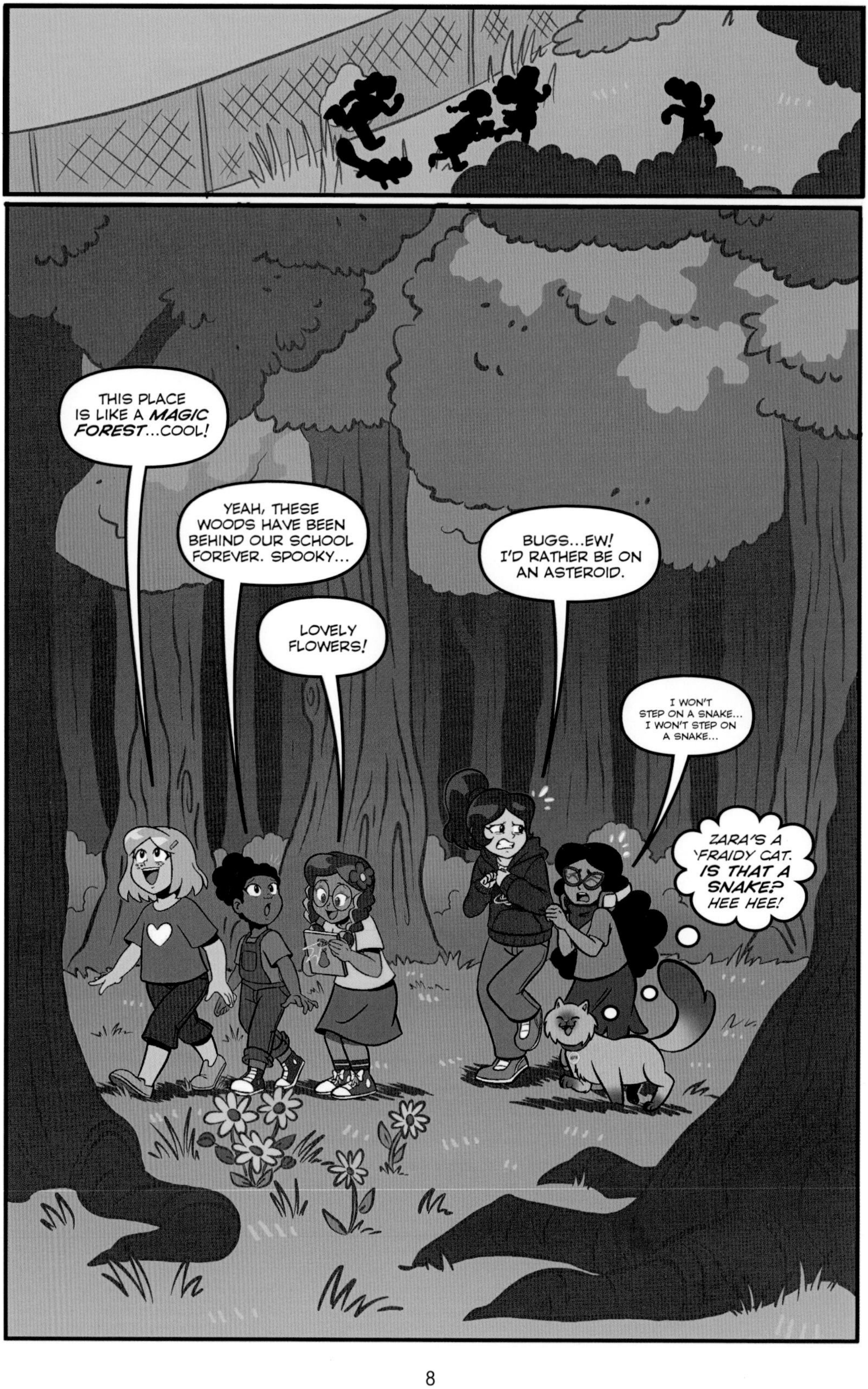
THIS PLACE IS LIKE A *MAGIC FOREST*...COOL!
YEAH, THESE WOODS HAVE BEEN BEHIND OUR SCHOOL FOREVER. SPOOKY...
LOVELY FLOWERS!
BUGS...EW! I'D RATHER BE ON AN ASTEROID.
I WON'T STEP ON A SNAKE... I WON'T STEP ON A SNAKE...
ZARA'S A 'FRAIDY CAT. ***IS THAT A SNAKE?*** *HEE HEE!*

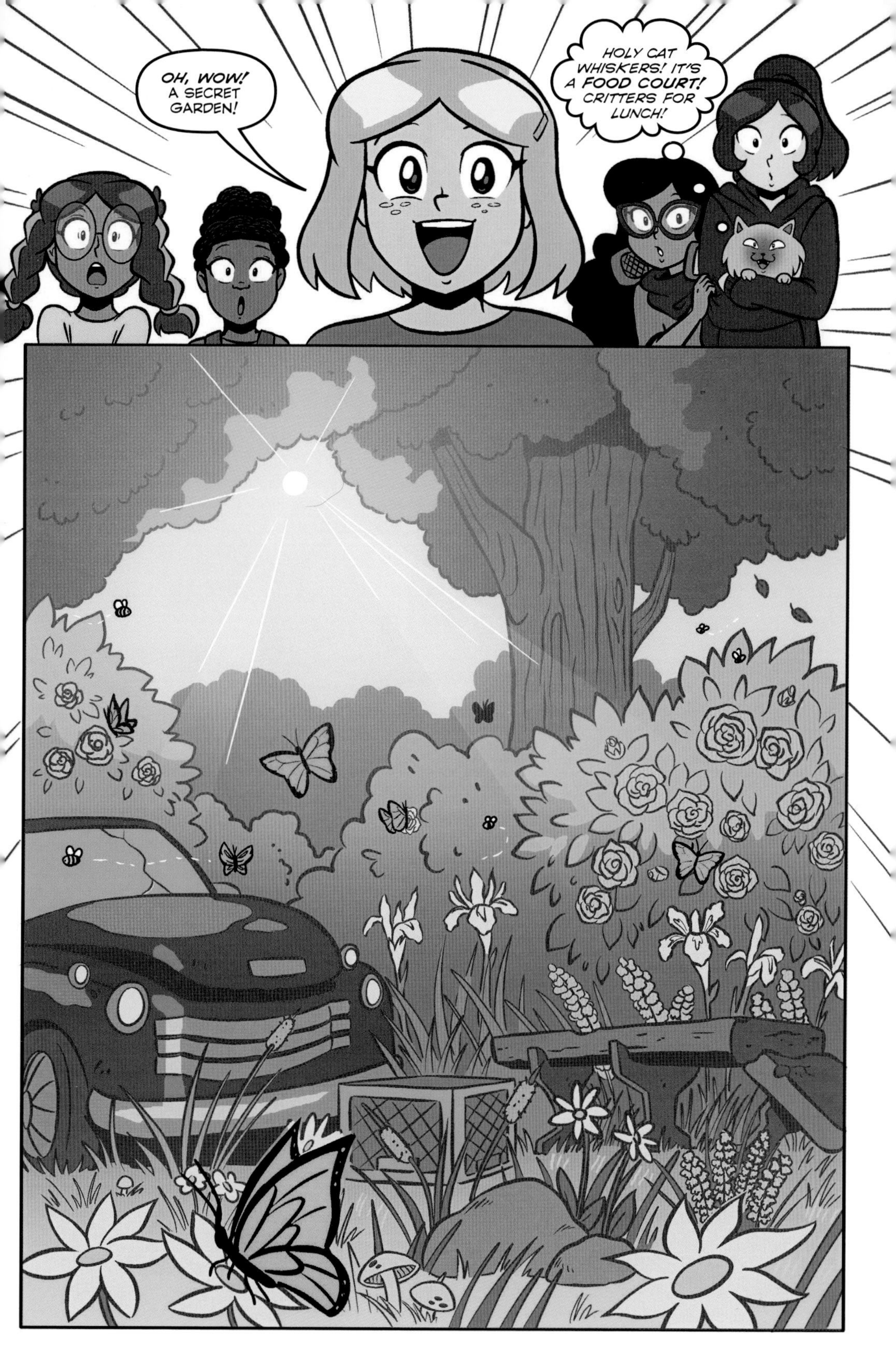
OH, WOW! A SECRET GARDEN!
HOLY CAT WHISKERS! IT'S A FOOD COURT! CRITTERS FOR LUNCH!

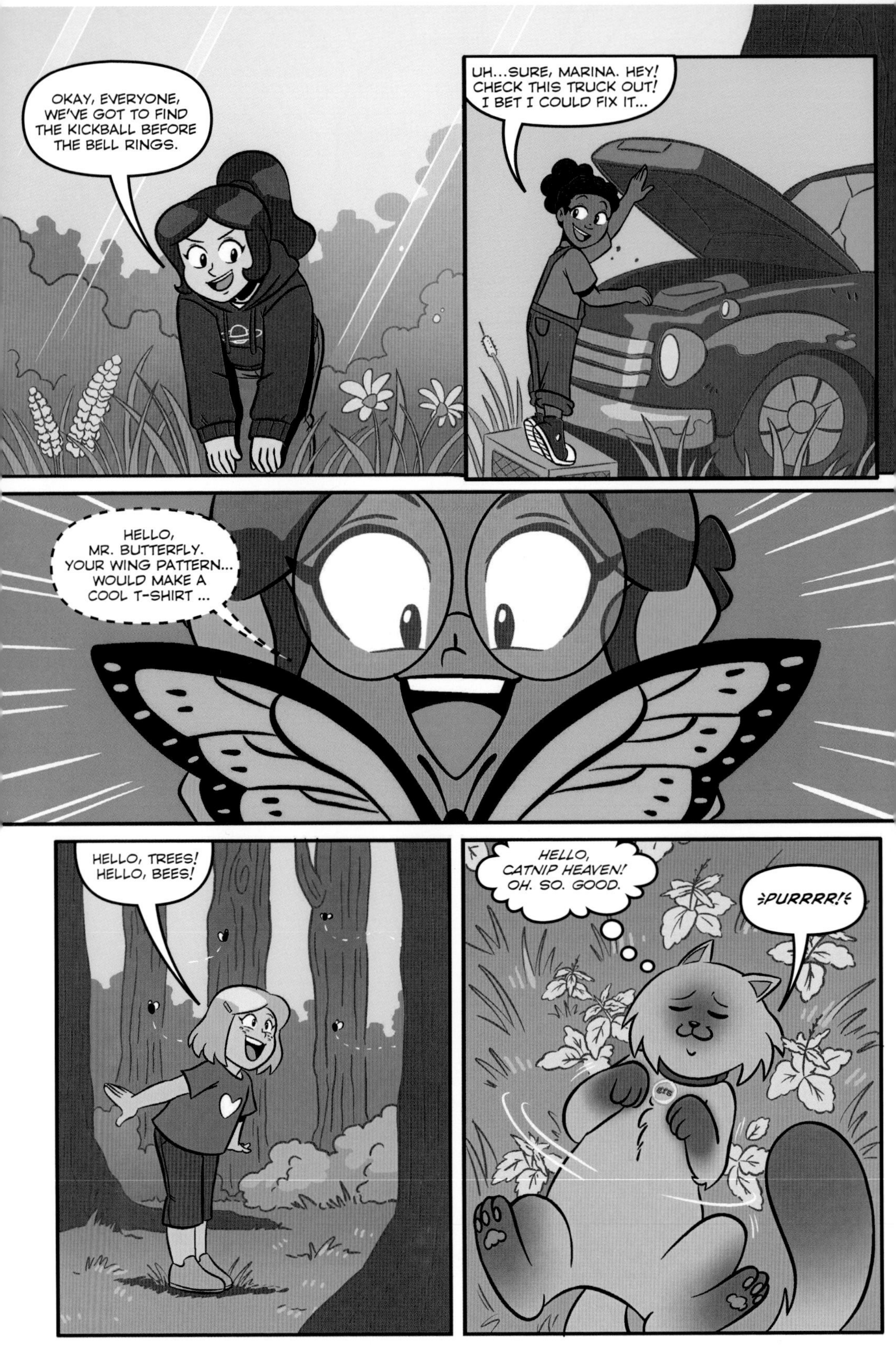
OKAY, EVERYONE, WE'VE GOT TO FIND THE KICKBALL BEFORE THE BELL RINGS.
UH...SURE, MARINA. HEY! CHECK THIS TRUCK OUT! I BET I COULD FIX IT...
HELLO, MR. BUTTERFLY. YOUR WING PATTERN... WOULD MAKE A COOL T-SHIRT ...
HELLO, TREES! HELLO, BEES!
HELLO, CATNIP HEAVEN! OH. SO. GOOD.
PURRRR!

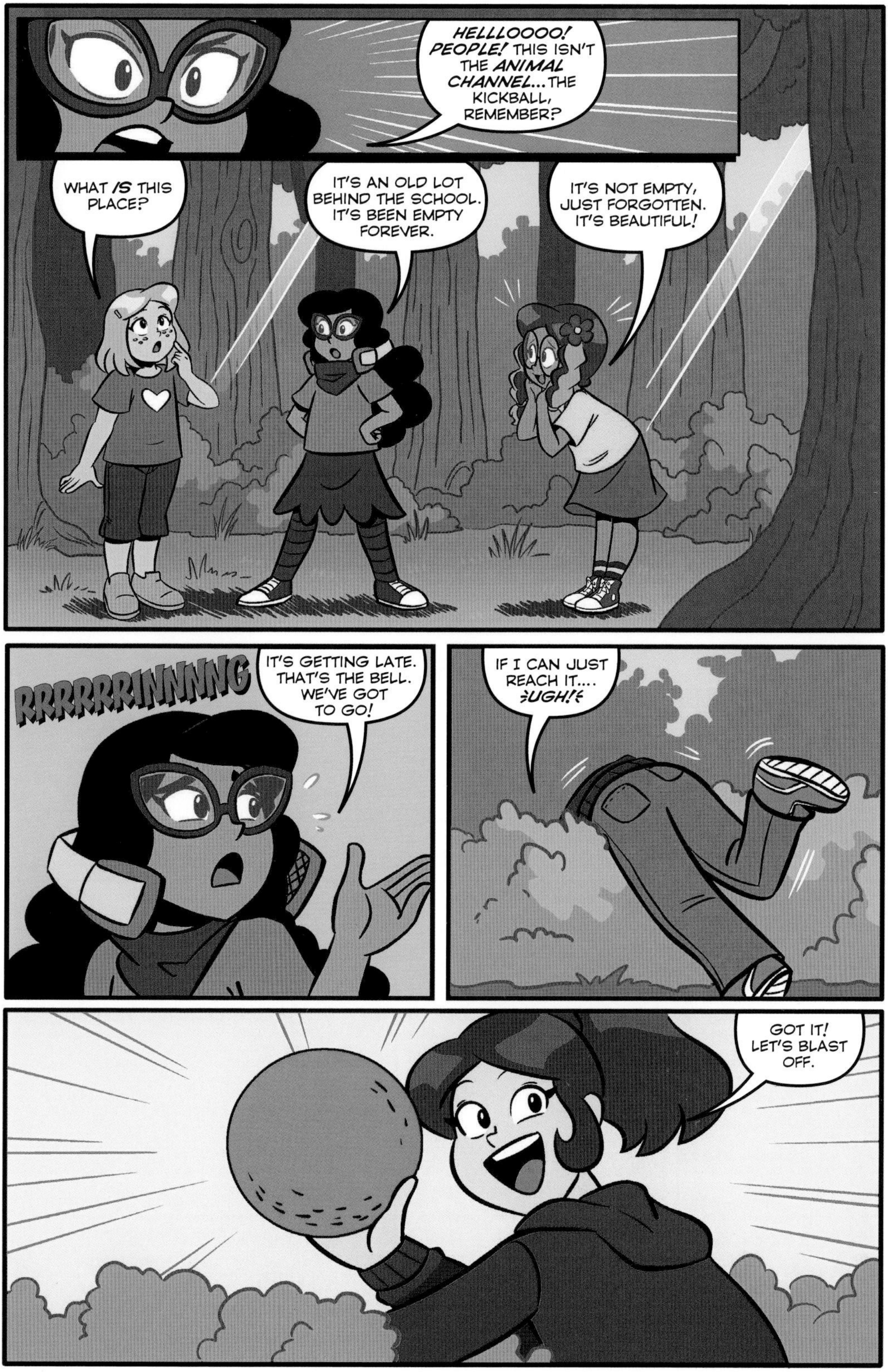
HELLLOOOO! PEOPLE! THIS ISN'T THE ANIMAL CHANNEL... THE KICKBALL, REMEMBER?
WHAT IS THIS PLACE?
IT'S AN OLD LOT BEHIND THE SCHOOL. IT'S BEEN EMPTY FOREVER.
IT'S NOT EMPTY, JUST FORGOTTEN. IT'S BEAUTIFUL!
RRRRRRINNNNG
IT'S GETTING LATE. THAT'S THE BELL. WE'VE GOT TO GO!
IF I CAN JUST REACH IT.... UGH!
GOT IT! LET'S BLAST OFF.

CHAPTER TWO:
CATERPILLARS, BUTTERFLIES, AND BEES! OH, MY!

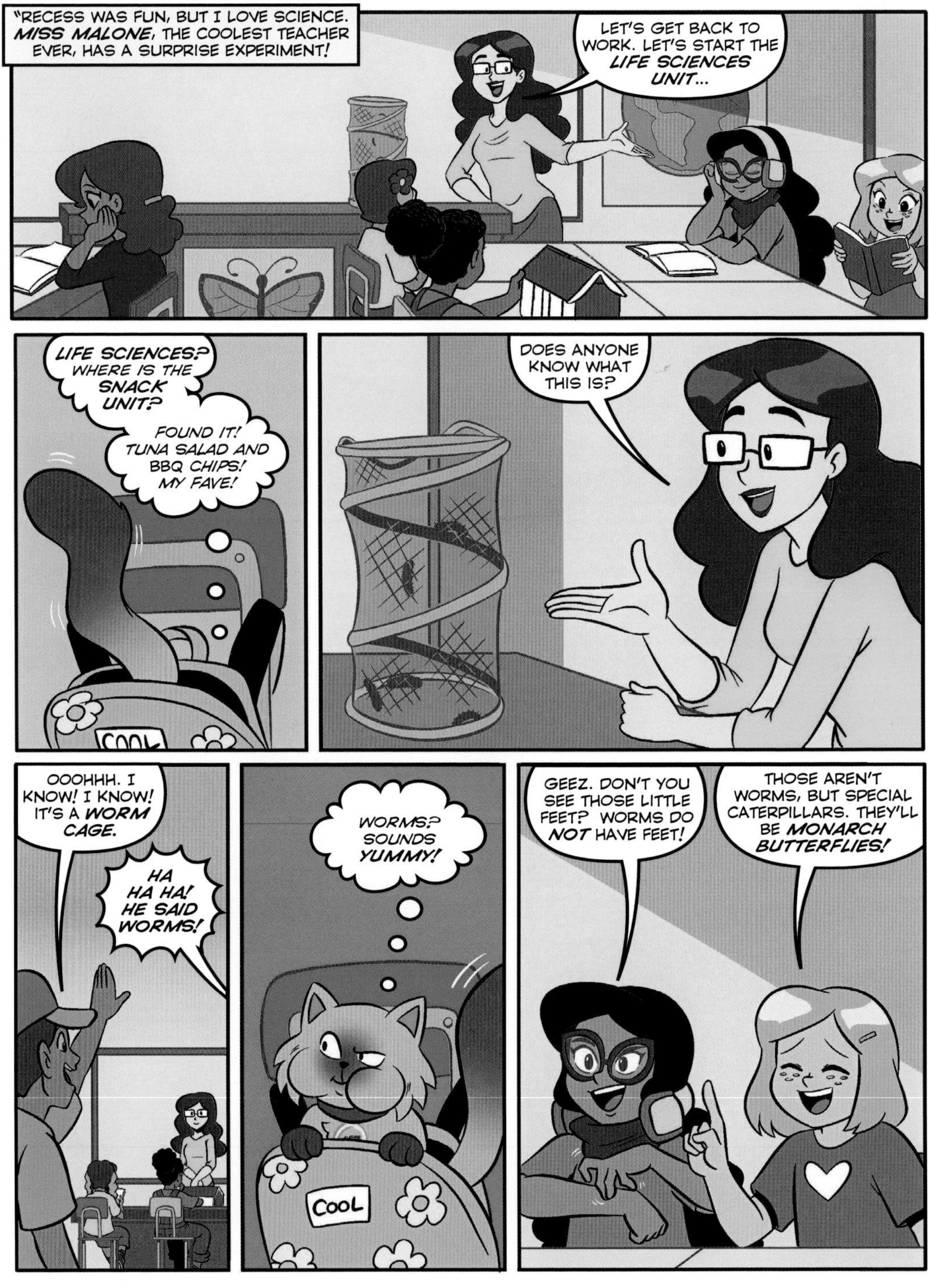
"RECESS WAS FUN, BUT I LOVE SCIENCE. MISS MALONE, THE COOLEST TEACHER EVER, HAS A SURPRISE EXPERIMENT!
LET'S GET BACK TO WORK. LET'S START THE LIFE SCIENCES UNIT...
LIFE SCIENCES? WHERE IS THE SNACK UNIT?
FOUND IT! TUNA SALAD AND BBQ CHIPS! MY FAVE!
COOL
DOES ANYONE KNOW WHAT THIS IS?
OOOHHH. I KNOW! I KNOW! IT'S A WORM CAGE.
HA HA HA! HE SAID WORMS!
WORMS? SOUNDS YUMMY!
COOL
GEEZ. DON'T YOU SEE THOSE LITTLE FEET? WORMS DO NOT HAVE FEET!
THOSE AREN'T WORMS, BUT SPECIAL CATERPILLARS. THEY'LL BE MONARCH BUTTERFLIES!

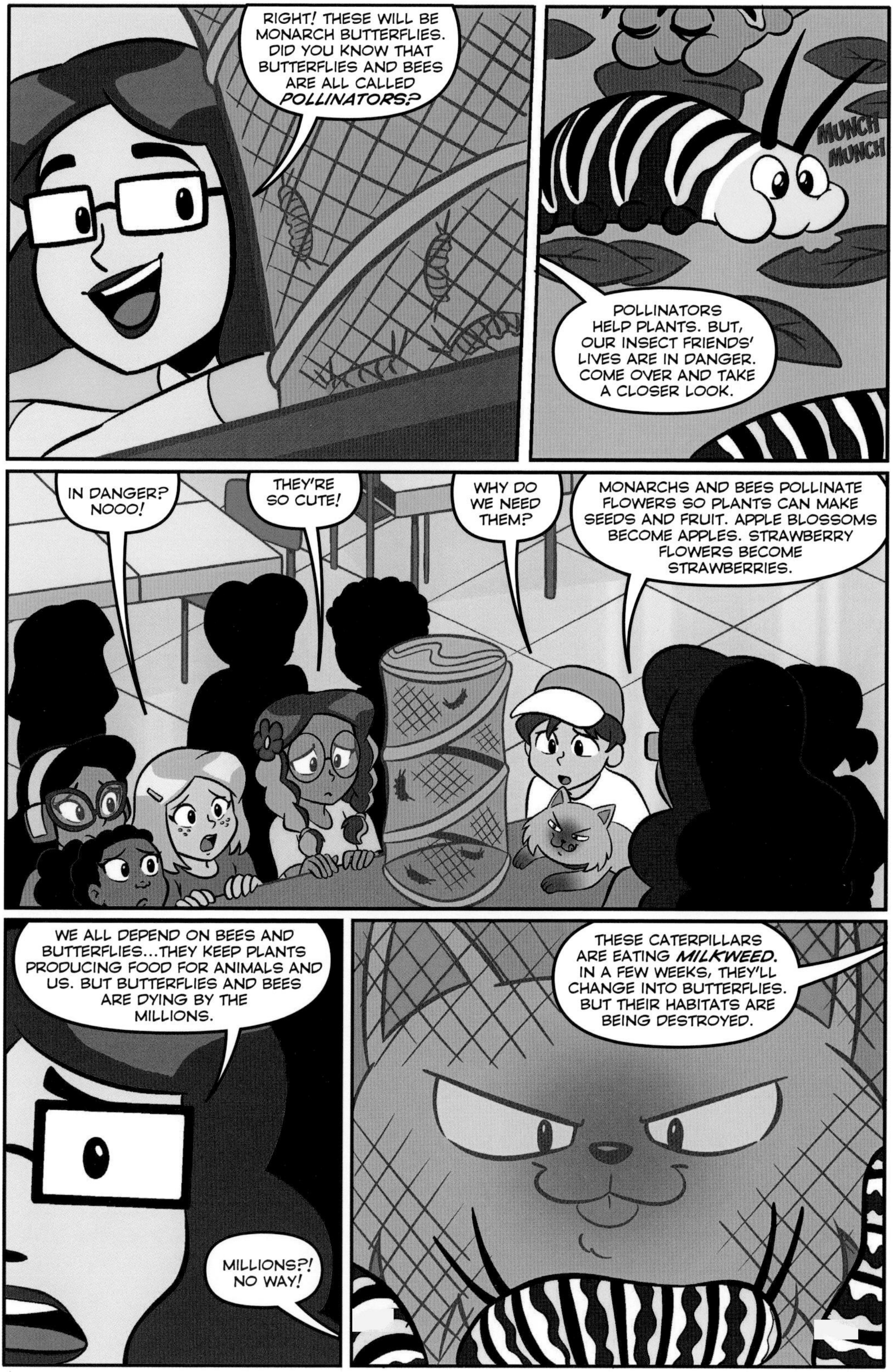
RIGHT! THESE WILL BE MONARCH BUTTERFLIES. DID YOU KNOW THAT BUTTERFLIES AND BEES ARE ALL CALLED *POLLINATORS?*
MUNCH MUNCH
POLLINATORS HELP PLANTS. BUT, OUR INSECT FRIENDS' LIVES ARE IN DANGER. COME OVER AND TAKE A CLOSER LOOK.
IN DANGER? NOOO!
THEY'RE SO CUTE!
WHY DO WE NEED THEM?
MONARCHS AND BEES POLLINATE FLOWERS SO PLANTS CAN MAKE SEEDS AND FRUIT. APPLE BLOSSOMS BECOME APPLES. STRAWBERRY FLOWERS BECOME STRAWBERRIES.
WE ALL DEPEND ON BEES AND BUTTERFLIES...THEY KEEP PLANTS PRODUCING FOOD FOR ANIMALS AND US. BUT BUTTERFLIES AND BEES ARE DYING BY THE MILLIONS.
MILLIONS?! NO WAY!
THESE CATERPILLARS ARE EATING *MILKWEED.* IN A FEW WEEKS, THEY'LL CHANGE INTO BUTTERFLIES. BUT THEIR HABITATS ARE BEING DESTROYED.

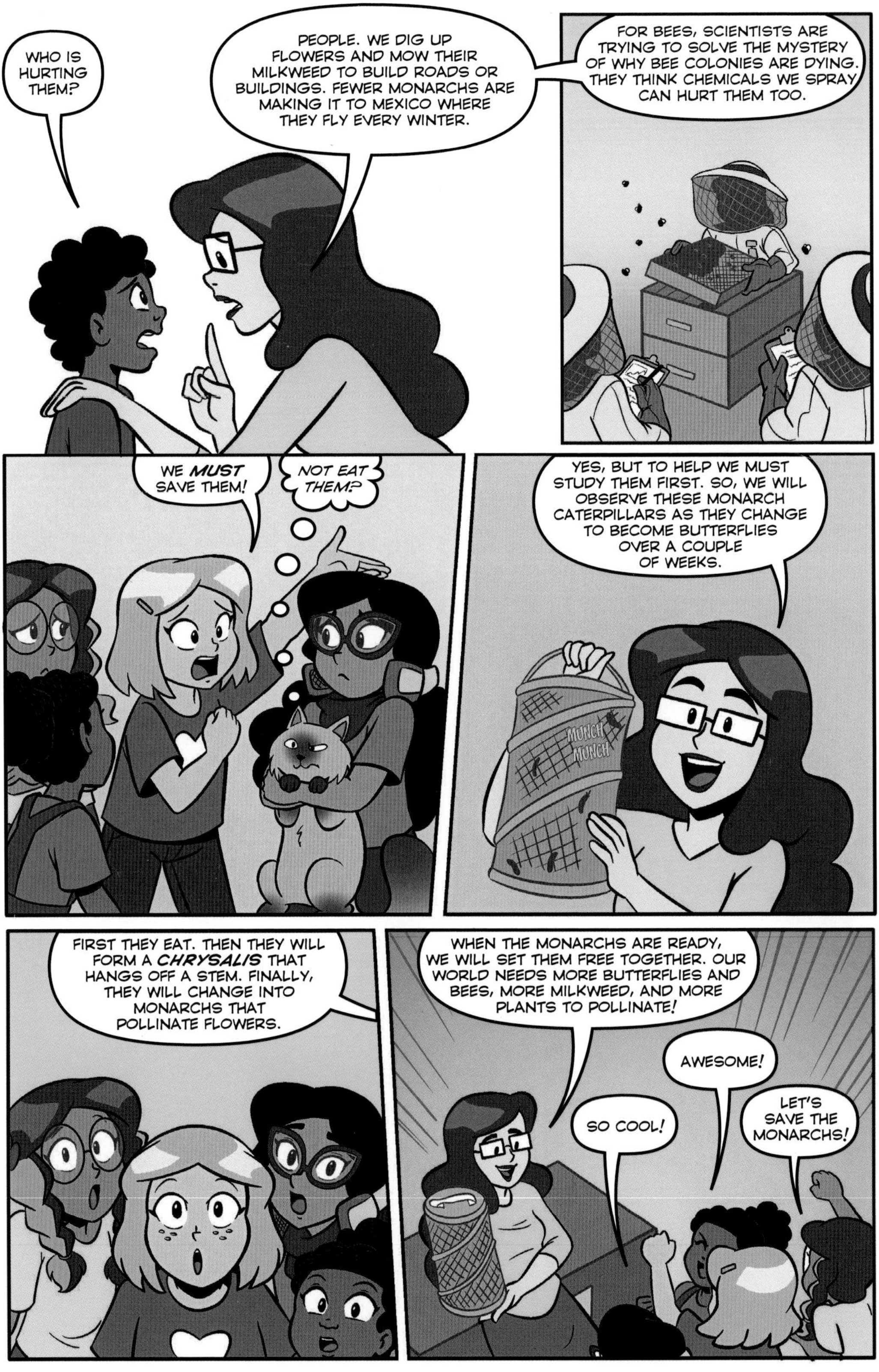
WHO IS HURTING THEM?
PEOPLE. WE DIG UP FLOWERS AND MOW THEIR MILKWEED TO BUILD ROADS OR BUILDINGS. FEWER MONARCHS ARE MAKING IT TO MEXICO WHERE THEY FLY EVERY WINTER.
FOR BEES, SCIENTISTS ARE TRYING TO SOLVE THE MYSTERY OF WHY BEE COLONIES ARE DYING. THEY THINK CHEMICALS WE SPRAY CAN HURT THEM TOO.
WE MUST SAVE THEM!
NOT EAT THEM?
YES, BUT TO HELP WE MUST STUDY THEM FIRST. SO, WE WILL OBSERVE THESE MONARCH CATERPILLARS AS THEY CHANGE TO BECOME BUTTERFLIES OVER A COUPLE OF WEEKS.
MUNCH MUNCH
FIRST THEY EAT. THEN THEY WILL FORM A CHRYSALIS THAT HANGS OFF A STEM. FINALLY, THEY WILL CHANGE INTO MONARCHS THAT POLLINATE FLOWERS.
WHEN THE MONARCHS ARE READY, WE WILL SET THEM FREE TOGETHER. OUR WORLD NEEDS MORE BUTTERFLIES AND BEES, MORE MILKWEED, AND MORE PLANTS TO POLLINATE!
AWESOME!
SO COOL!
LET'S SAVE THE MONARCHS!

CHAPTER THREE: A TOTALLY TUBULAR CATERPILLAR

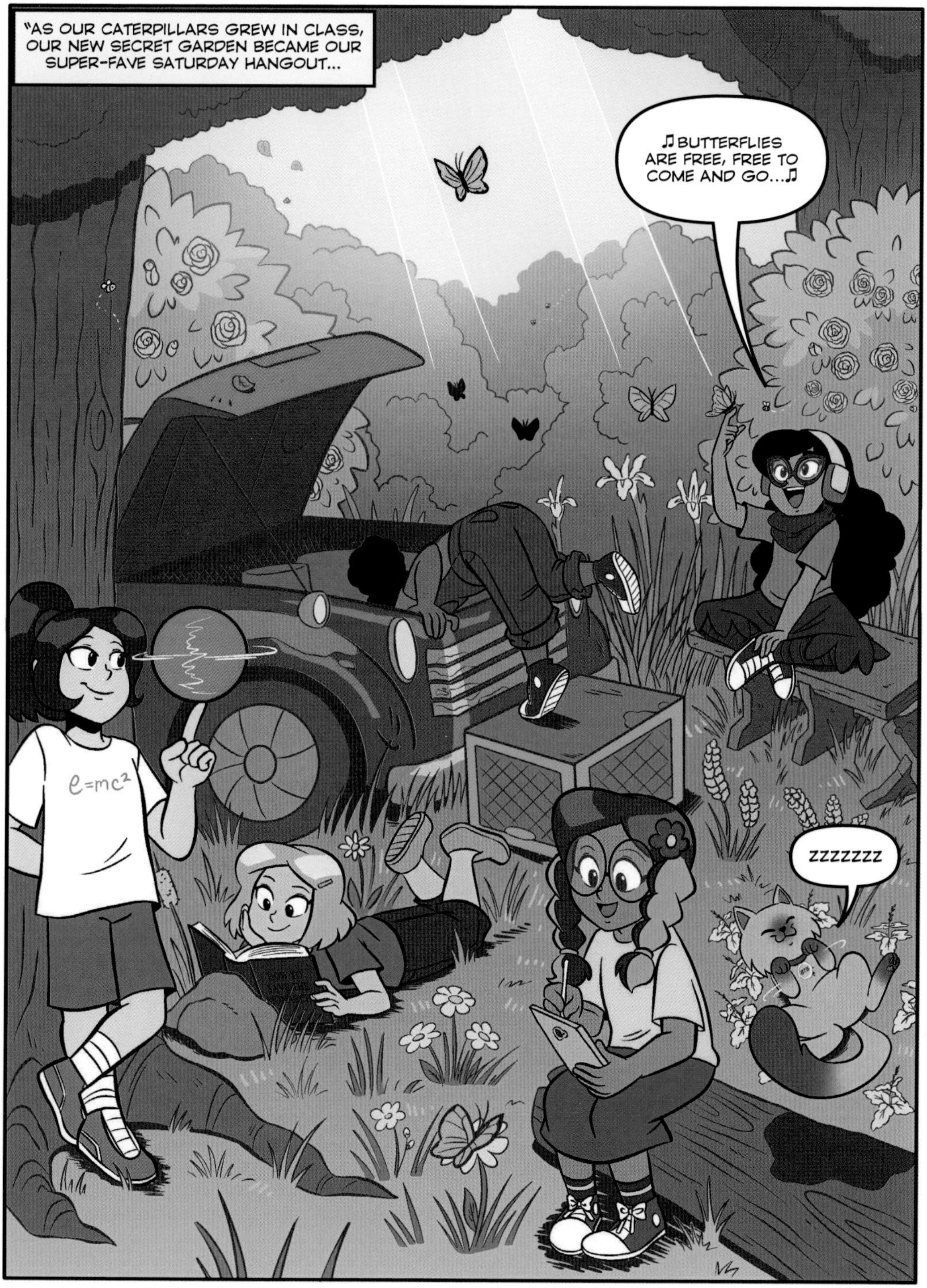
"AS OUR CATERPILLARS GREW IN CLASS, OUR NEW SECRET GARDEN BECAME OUR SUPER-FAVE SATURDAY HANGOUT...
♫ BUTTERFLIES ARE FREE, FREE TO COME AND GO...♫
e=mc²
ZZZZZZZ

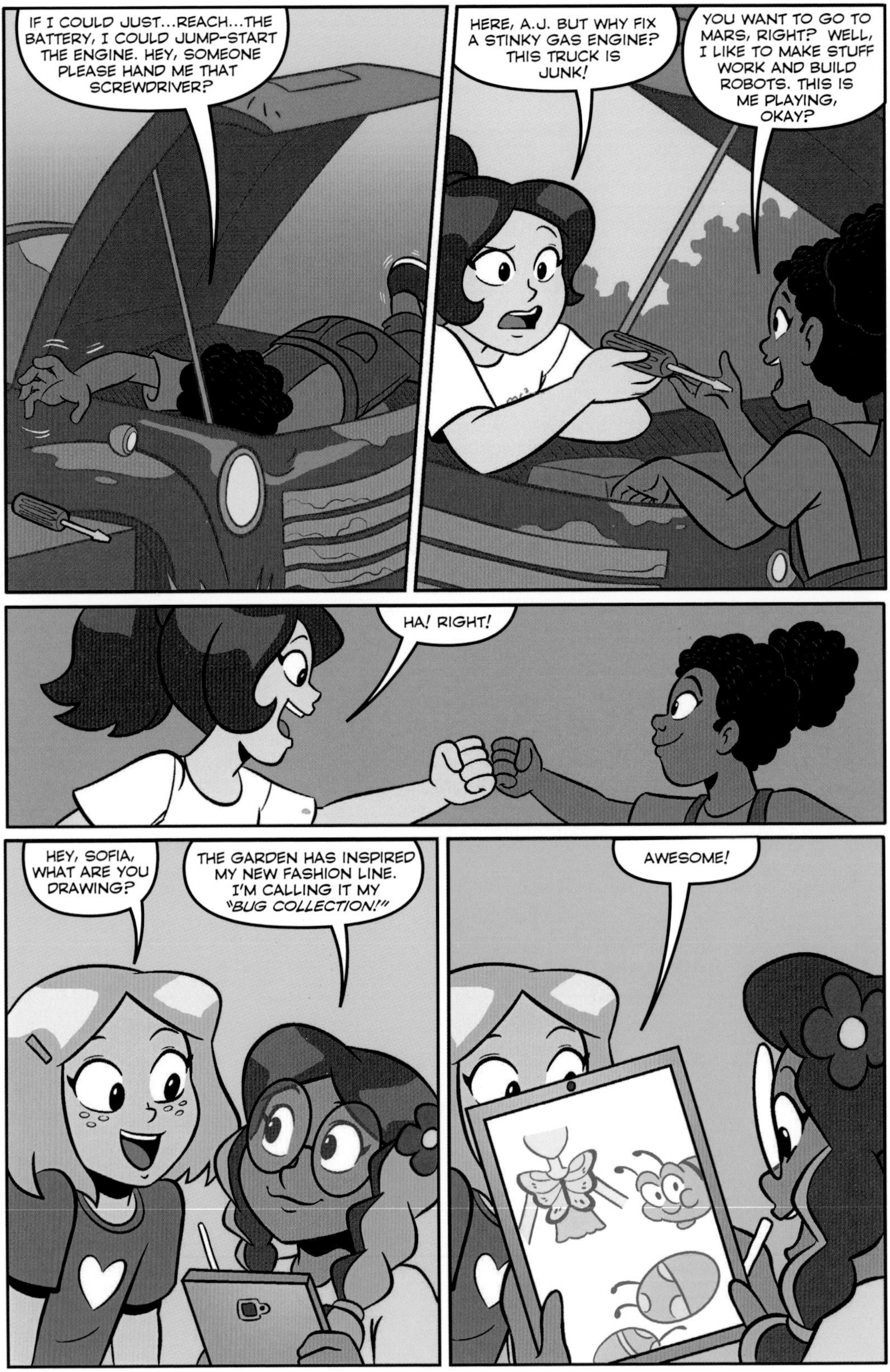
IF I COULD JUST...REACH...THE BATTERY, I COULD JUMP-START THE ENGINE. HEY, SOMEONE PLEASE HAND ME THAT SCREWDRIVER?
HERE, A.J. BUT WHY FIX A STINKY GAS ENGINE? THIS TRUCK IS JUNK!
YOU WANT TO GO TO MARS, RIGHT? WELL, I LIKE TO MAKE STUFF WORK AND BUILD ROBOTS. THIS IS ME PLAYING, OKAY?
HA! RIGHT!
HEY, SOFIA, WHAT ARE YOU DRAWING?
THE GARDEN HAS INSPIRED MY NEW FASHION LINE. I'M CALLING IT MY "BUG COLLECTION!"
AWESOME!

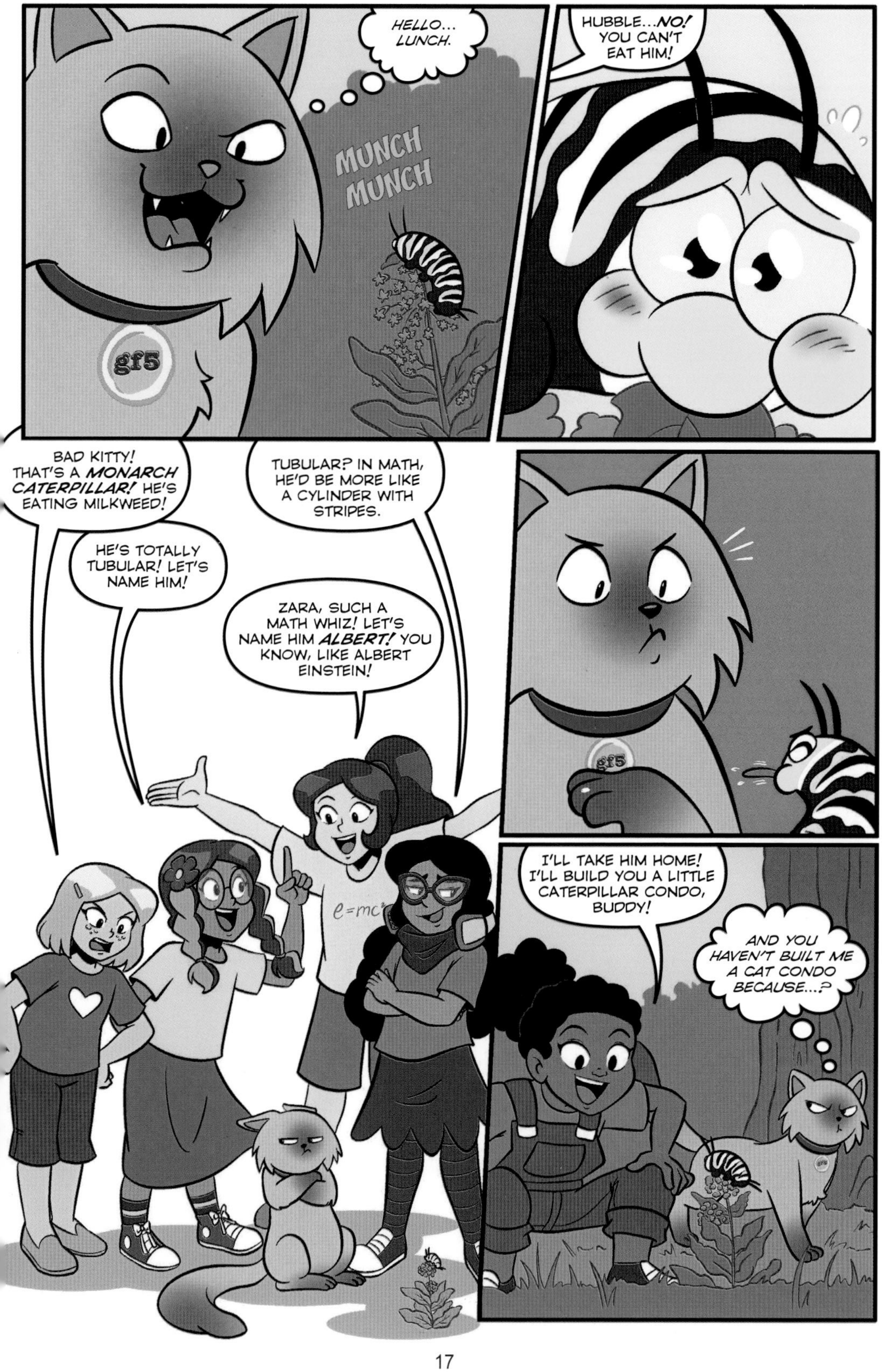
HELLO... LUNCH.
MUNCH MUNCH
HUBBLE...NO! YOU CAN'T EAT HIM!
BAD KITTY! THAT'S A MONARCH CATERPILLAR! HE'S EATING MILKWEED!
HE'S TOTALLY TUBULAR! LET'S NAME HIM!
TUBULAR? IN MATH, HE'D BE MORE LIKE A CYLINDER WITH STRIPES.
ZARA, SUCH A MATH WHIZ! LET'S NAME HIM ALBERT! YOU KNOW, LIKE ALBERT EINSTEIN!
e=mc²
I'LL TAKE HIM HOME! I'LL BUILD YOU A LITTLE CATERPILLAR CONDO, BUDDY!
AND YOU HAVEN'T BUILT ME A CAT CONDO BECAUSE...?

CHAPTER FOUR: GOING BUGGY

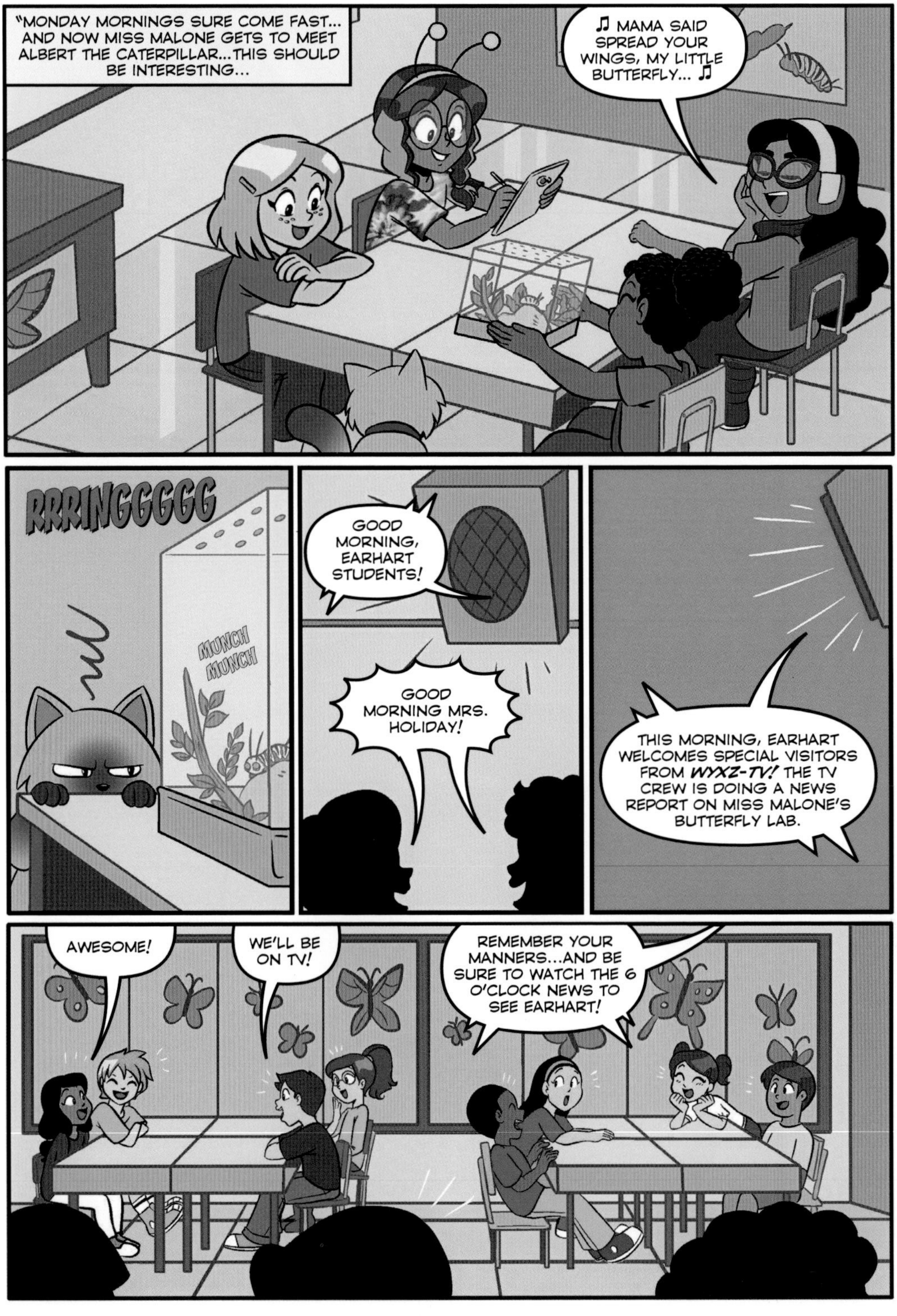
"MONDAY MORNINGS SURE COME FAST... AND NOW MISS MALONE GETS TO MEET ALBERT THE CATERPILLAR...THIS SHOULD BE INTERESTING...
♫ MAMA SAID SPREAD YOUR WINGS, MY LITTLE BUTTERFLY... ♫
RRRINGGGGG
MUNCH MUNCH
GOOD MORNING, EARHART STUDENTS!
GOOD MORNING MRS. HOLIDAY!
THIS MORNING, EARHART WELCOMES SPECIAL VISITORS FROM WYXZ-TV! THE TV CREW IS DOING A NEWS REPORT ON MISS MALONE'S BUTTERFLY LAB.
AWESOME!
WE'LL BE ON TV!
REMEMBER YOUR MANNERS...AND BE SURE TO WATCH THE 6 O'CLOCK NEWS TO SEE EARHART!

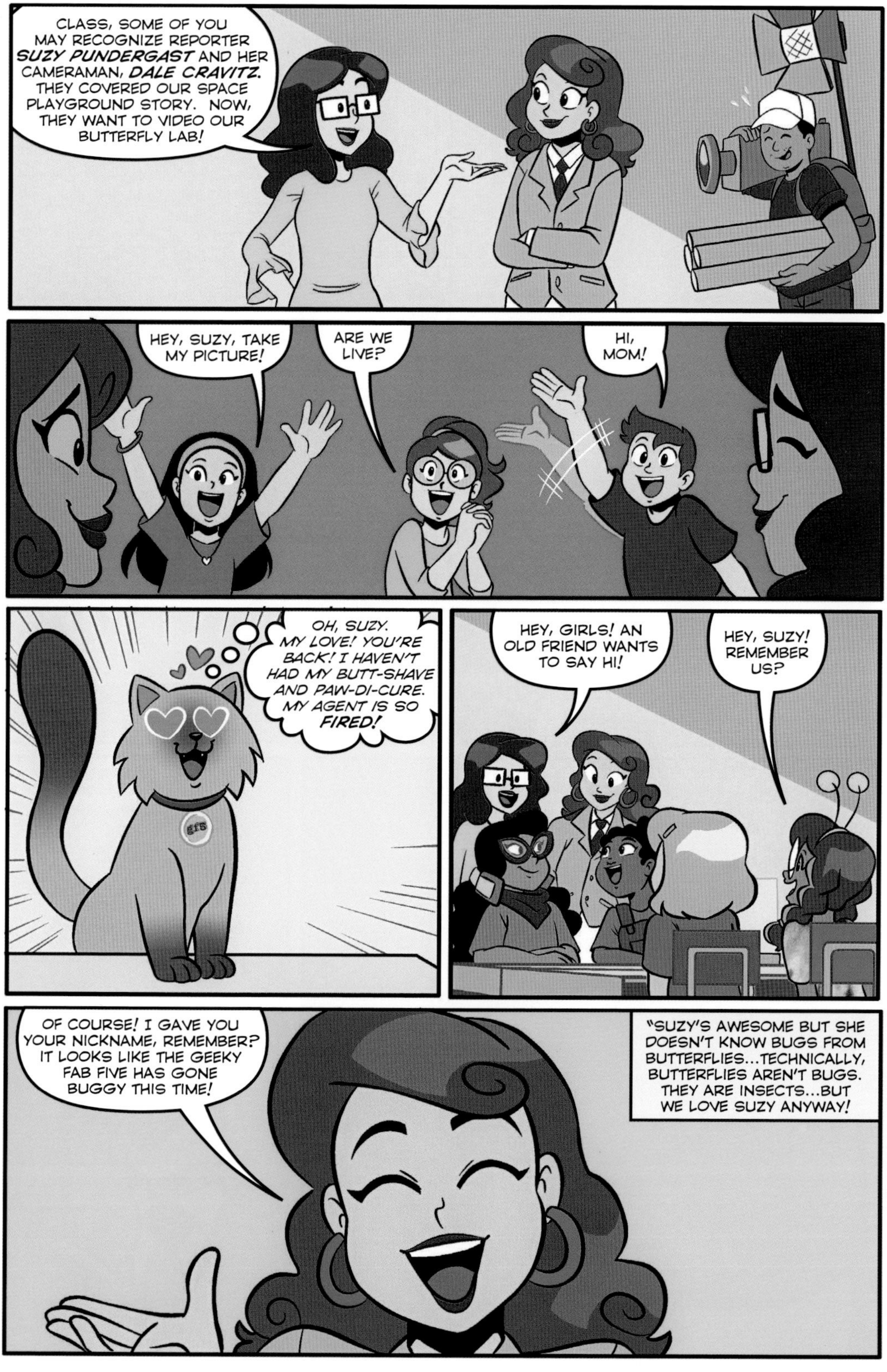

CLASS, SOME OF YOU MAY RECOGNIZE REPORTER SUZY PUNDERGAST AND HER CAMERAMAN, DALE CRAVITZ. THEY COVERED OUR SPACE PLAYGROUND STORY. NOW, THEY WANT TO VIDEO OUR BUTTERFLY LAB!
HEY, SUZY, TAKE MY PICTURE!
ARE WE LIVE?
HI, MOM!
OH, SUZY. MY LOVE! YOU'RE BACK! I HAVEN'T HAD MY BUTT-SHAVE AND PAW-DI-CURE. MY AGENT IS SO FIRED!
HEY, GIRLS! AN OLD FRIEND WANTS TO SAY HI!
HEY, SUZY! REMEMBER US?
OF COURSE! I GAVE YOU YOUR NICKNAME, REMEMBER? IT LOOKS LIKE THE GEEKY FAB FIVE HAS GONE BUGGY THIS TIME!
"SUZY'S AWESOME BUT SHE DOESN'T KNOW BUGS FROM BUTTERFLIES...TECHNICALLY, BUTTERFLIES AREN'T BUGS. THEY ARE INSECTS...BUT WE LOVE SUZY ANYWAY!

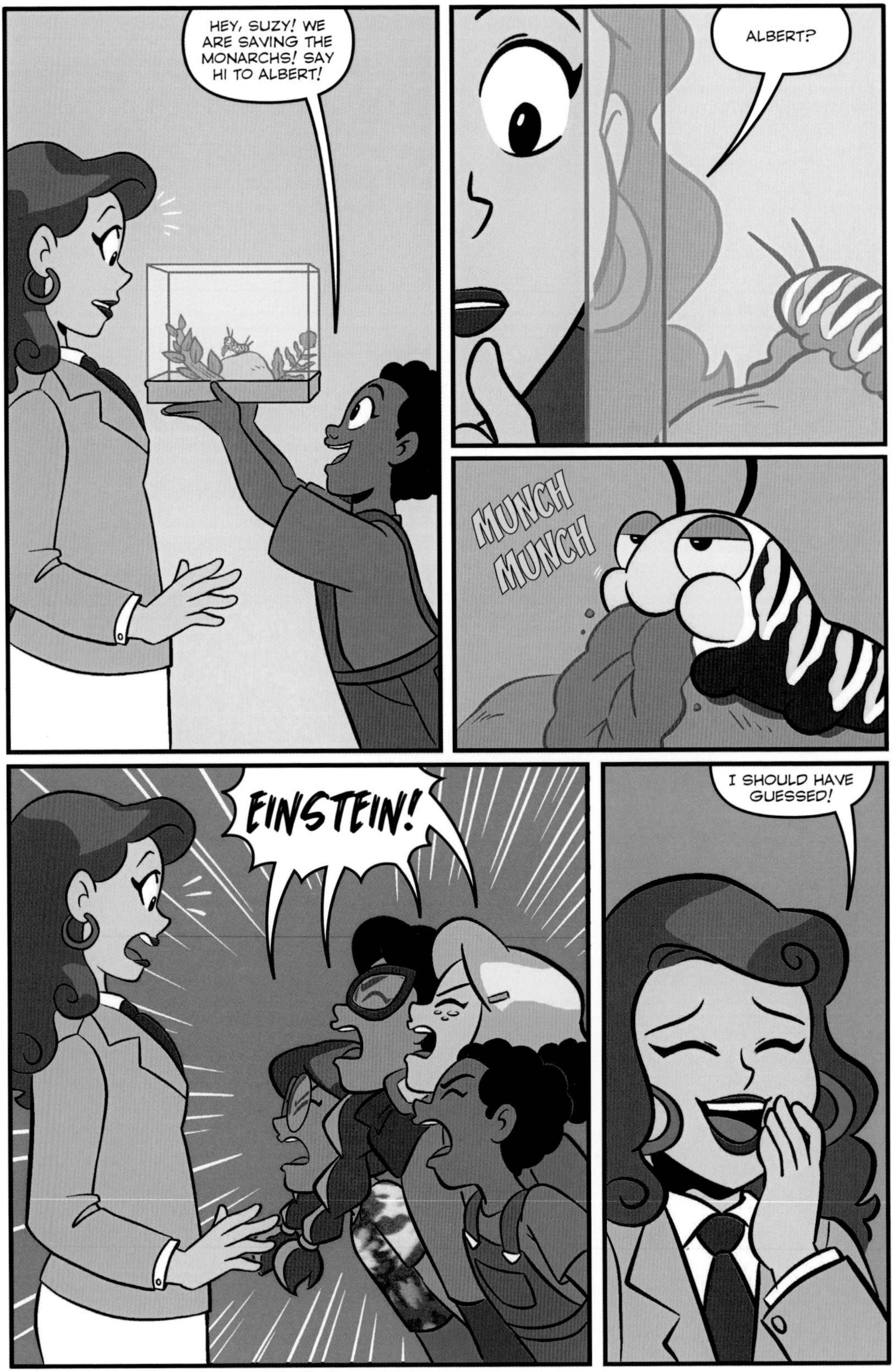
HEY, SUZY! WE ARE SAVING THE MONARCHS! SAY HI TO ALBERT!
ALBERT?
MUNCH MUNCH
EINSTEIN!
I SHOULD HAVE GUESSED!

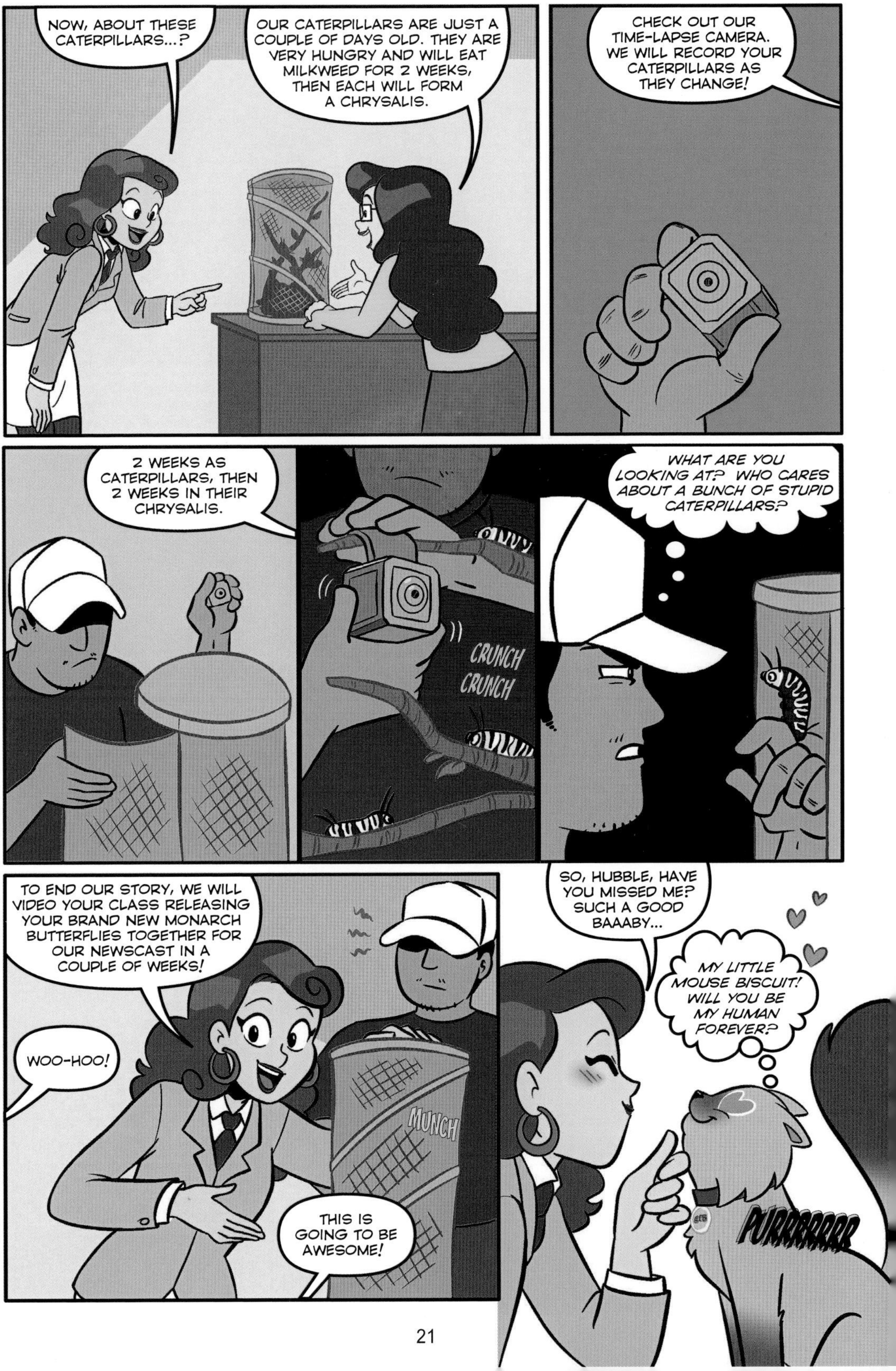
NOW, ABOUT THESE CATERPILLARS...?
OUR CATERPILLARS ARE JUST A COUPLE OF DAYS OLD. THEY ARE VERY HUNGRY AND WILL EAT MILKWEED FOR 2 WEEKS, THEN EACH WILL FORM A CHRYSALIS.
CHECK OUT OUR TIME-LAPSE CAMERA. WE WILL RECORD YOUR CATERPILLARS AS THEY CHANGE!
2 WEEKS AS CATERPILLARS, THEN 2 WEEKS IN THEIR CHRYSALIS.
CRUNCH
CRUNCH
WHAT ARE YOU LOOKING AT? WHO CARES ABOUT A BUNCH OF STUPID CATERPILLARS?
TO END OUR STORY, WE WILL VIDEO YOUR CLASS RELEASING YOUR BRAND NEW MONARCH BUTTERFLIES TOGETHER FOR OUR NEWSCAST IN A COUPLE OF WEEKS!
WOO-HOO!
MUNCH
THIS IS GOING TO BE AWESOME!
SO, HUBBLE, HAVE YOU MISSED ME? SUCH A GOOD BAAABY...
MY LITTLE MOUSE BISCUIT! WILL YOU BE MY HUMAN FOREVER?
PURRRRRRR

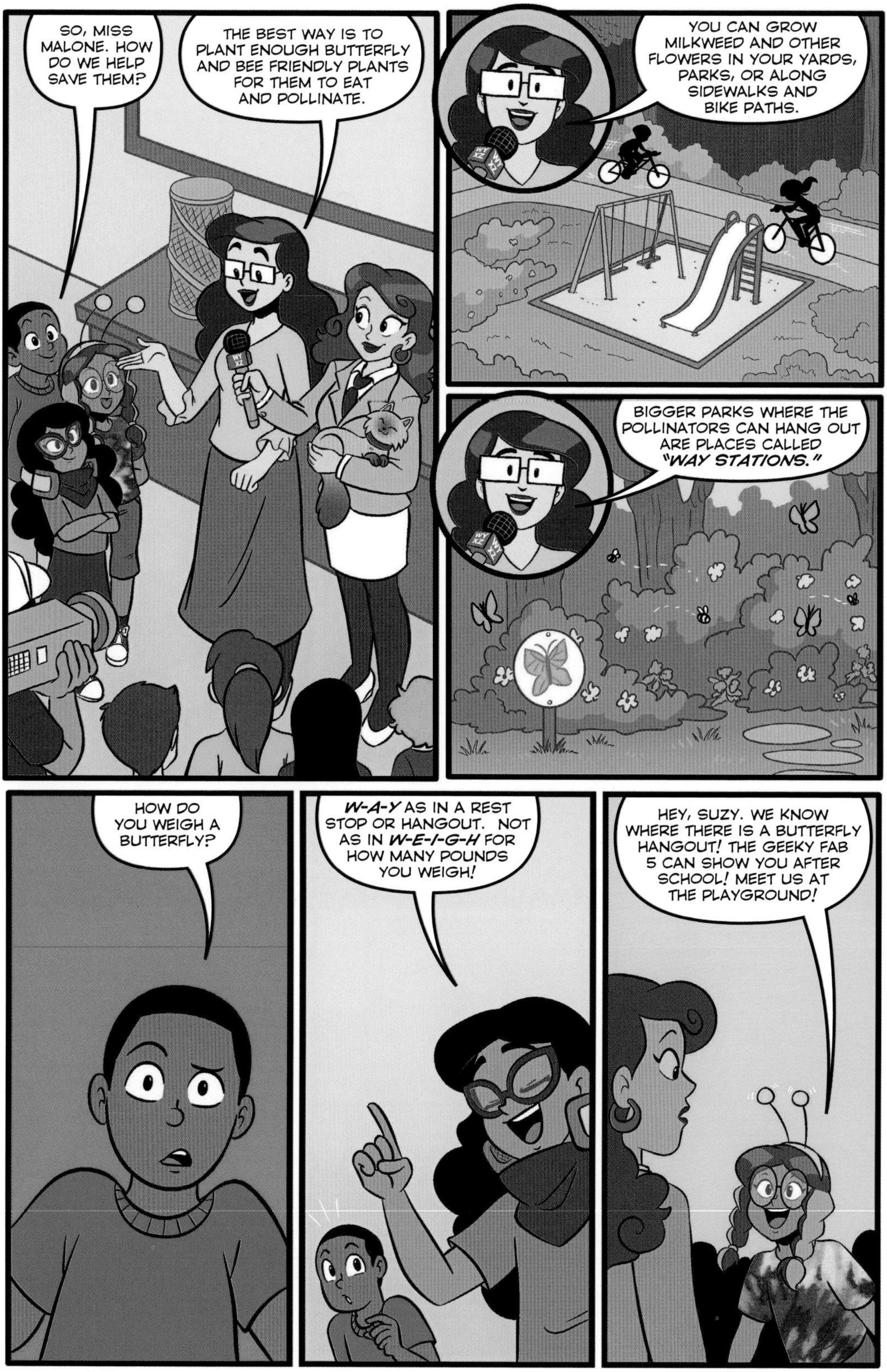
SO, MISS MALONE. HOW DO WE HELP SAVE THEM?
THE BEST WAY IS TO PLANT ENOUGH BUTTERFLY AND BEE FRIENDLY PLANTS FOR THEM TO EAT AND POLLINATE.
YOU CAN GROW MILKWEED AND OTHER FLOWERS IN YOUR YARDS, PARKS, OR ALONG SIDEWALKS AND BIKE PATHS.
BIGGER PARKS WHERE THE POLLINATORS CAN HANG OUT ARE PLACES CALLED *"WAY STATIONS."*
HOW DO YOU WEIGH A BUTTERFLY?
W-A-Y AS IN A REST STOP OR HANGOUT. NOT AS IN *W-E-I-G-H* FOR HOW MANY POUNDS YOU WEIGH!
HEY, SUZY. WE KNOW WHERE THERE IS A BUTTERFLY HANGOUT! THE GEEKY FAB 5 CAN SHOW YOU AFTER SCHOOL! MEET US AT THE PLAYGROUND!

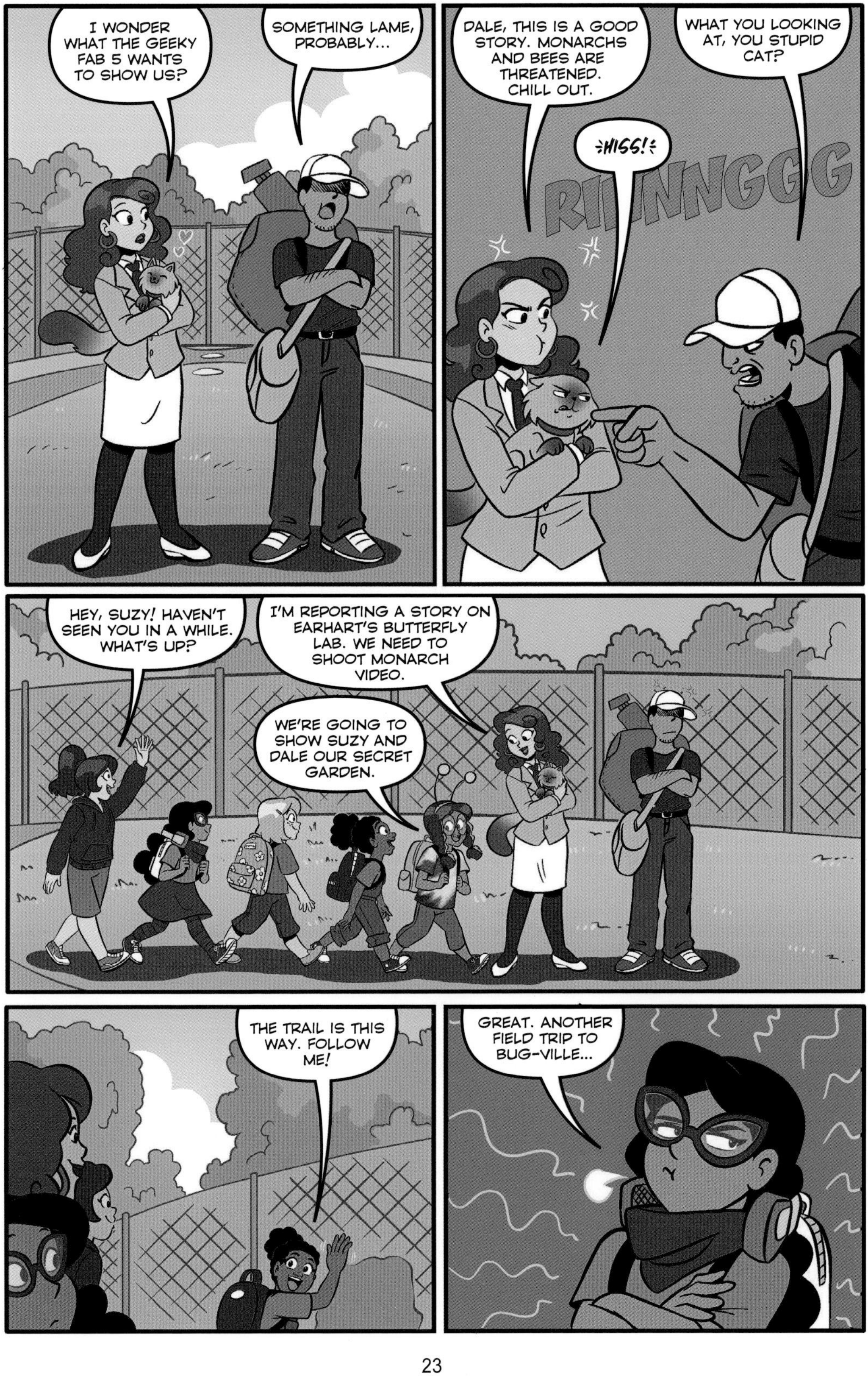
I WONDER WHAT THE GEEKY FAB 5 WANTS TO SHOW US?
SOMETHING LAME, PROBABLY...
DALE, THIS IS A GOOD STORY. MONARCHS AND BEES ARE THREATENED. CHILL OUT.
WHAT YOU LOOKING AT, YOU STUPID CAT?
HISS!
RIINNGGG
HEY, SUZY! HAVEN'T SEEN YOU IN A WHILE. WHAT'S UP?
I'M REPORTING A STORY ON EARHART'S BUTTERFLY LAB. WE NEED TO SHOOT MONARCH VIDEO.
WE'RE GOING TO SHOW SUZY AND DALE OUR SECRET GARDEN.
THE TRAIL IS THIS WAY. FOLLOW ME!
GREAT. ANOTHER FIELD TRIP TO BUG-VILLE...

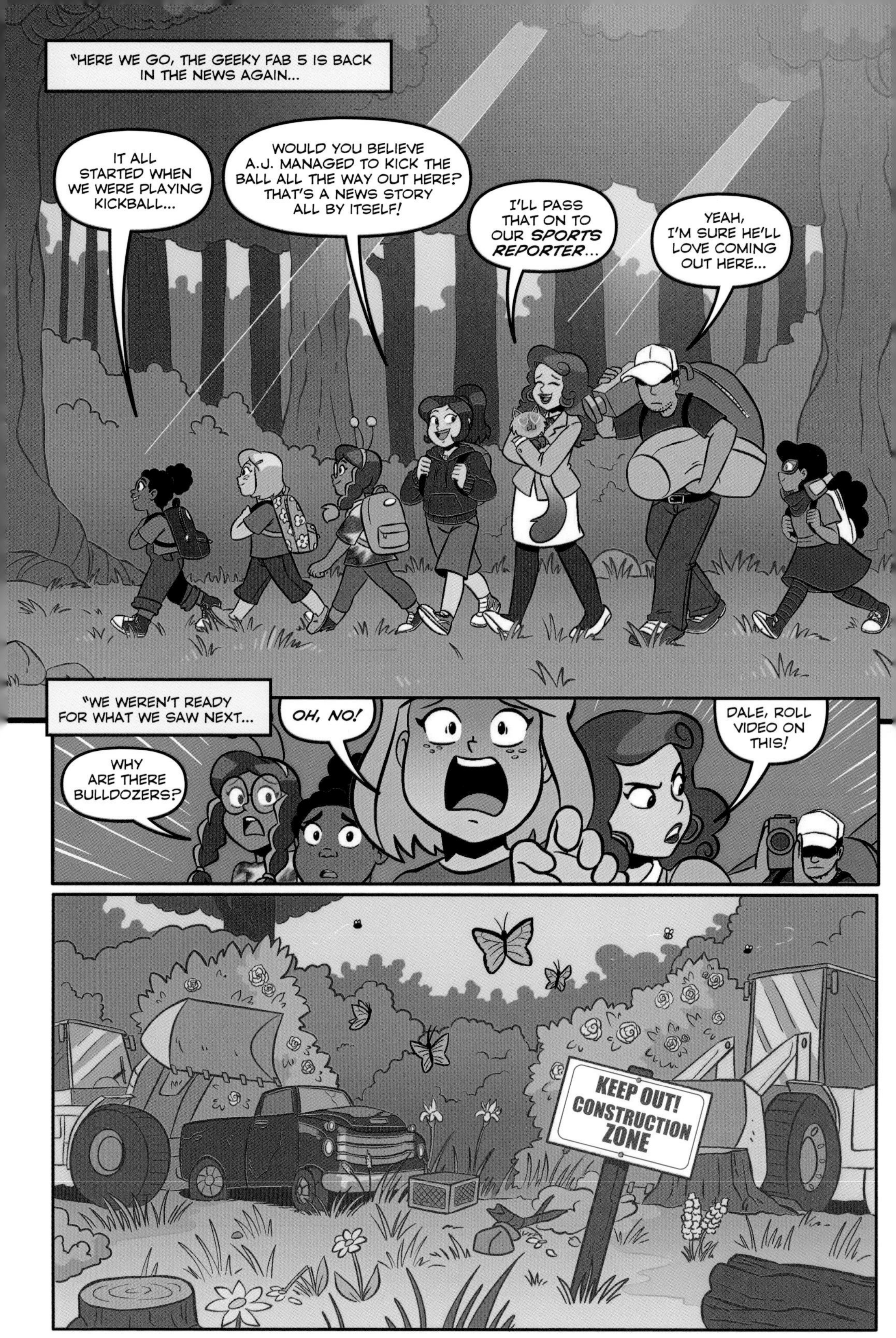
"HERE WE GO, THE GEEKY FAB 5 IS BACK IN THE NEWS AGAIN...
IT ALL STARTED WHEN WE WERE PLAYING KICKBALL...
WOULD YOU BELIEVE A.J. MANAGED TO KICK THE BALL ALL THE WAY OUT HERE? THAT'S A NEWS STORY ALL BY ITSELF!
I'LL PASS THAT ON TO OUR *SPORTS REPORTER*...
YEAH, I'M SURE HE'LL LOVE COMING OUT HERE...
"WE WEREN'T READY FOR WHAT WE SAW NEXT...
WHY ARE THERE BULLDOZERS?
OH, NO!
DALE, ROLL VIDEO ON THIS!
KEEP OUT! CONSTRUCTION ZONE

CHAPTER FIVE: DOUBLE TROUBLE FOR THE GARDEN AND HUBBLE

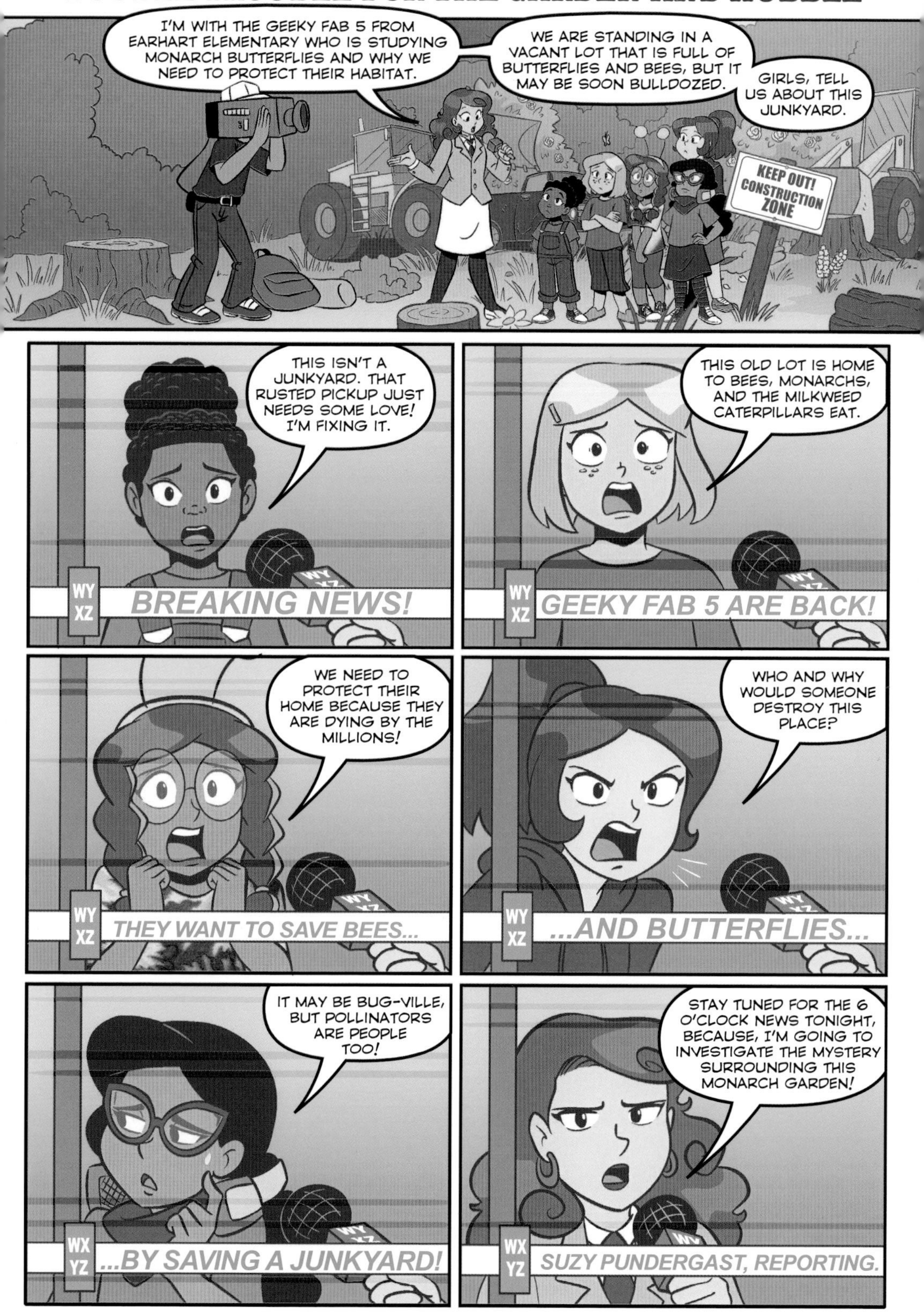

I'M WITH THE GEEKY FAB 5 FROM EARHART ELEMENTARY WHO IS STUDYING MONARCH BUTTERFLIES AND WHY WE NEED TO PROTECT THEIR HABITAT.
WE ARE STANDING IN A VACANT LOT THAT IS FULL OF BUTTERFLIES AND BEES, BUT IT MAY BE SOON BULLDOZED.
GIRLS, TELL US ABOUT THIS JUNKYARD.
KEEP OUT! CONSTRUCTION ZONE
THIS ISN'T A JUNKYARD. THAT RUSTED PICKUP JUST NEEDS SOME LOVE! I'M FIXING IT.
WY XZ
BREAKING NEWS!
THIS OLD LOT IS HOME TO BEES, MONARCHS, AND THE MILKWEED CATERPILLARS EAT.
WY XZ
GEEKY FAB 5 ARE BACK!
WE NEED TO PROTECT THEIR HOME BECAUSE THEY ARE DYING BY THE MILLIONS!
WY XZ
THEY WANT TO SAVE BEES...
WHO AND WHY WOULD SOMEONE DESTROY THIS PLACE?
WY XZ
...AND BUTTERFLIES...
IT MAY BE BUG-VILLE, BUT POLLINATORS ARE PEOPLE TOO!
WX YZ
...BY SAVING A JUNKYARD!
STAY TUNED FOR THE 6 O'CLOCK NEWS TONIGHT, BECAUSE, I'M GOING TO INVESTIGATE THE MYSTERY SURROUNDING THIS MONARCH GARDEN!
WX YZ
SUZY PUNDERGAST, REPORTING.

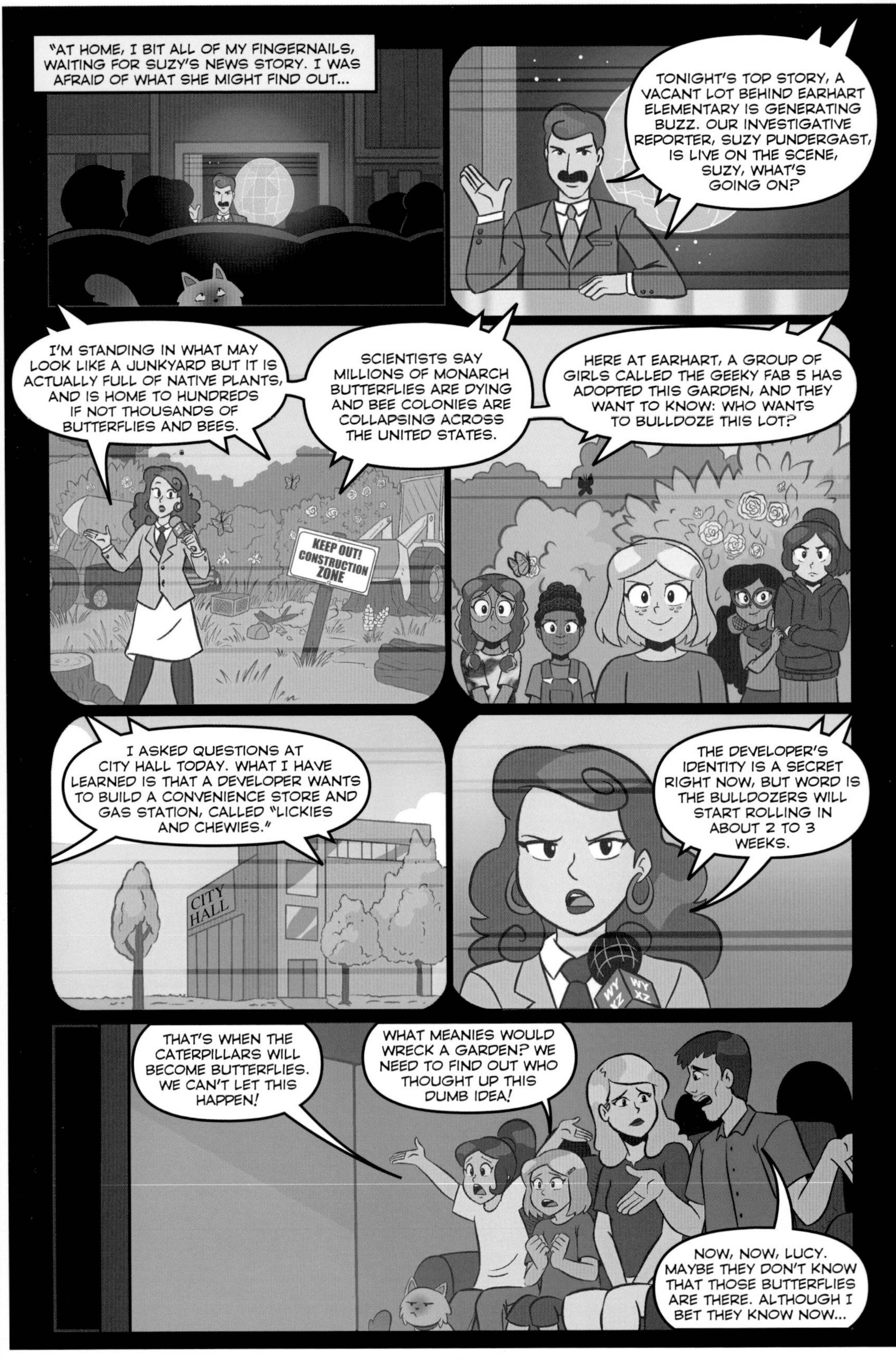
"AT HOME, I BIT ALL OF MY FINGERNAILS, WAITING FOR SUZY'S NEWS STORY. I WAS AFRAID OF WHAT SHE MIGHT FIND OUT...
TONIGHT'S TOP STORY, A VACANT LOT BEHIND EARHART ELEMENTARY IS GENERATING BUZZ. OUR INVESTIGATIVE REPORTER, SUZY PUNDERGAST, IS LIVE ON THE SCENE. SUZY, WHAT'S GOING ON?
I'M STANDING IN WHAT MAY LOOK LIKE A JUNKYARD BUT IT IS ACTUALLY FULL OF NATIVE PLANTS, AND IS HOME TO HUNDREDS IF NOT THOUSANDS OF BUTTERFLIES AND BEES.
SCIENTISTS SAY MILLIONS OF MONARCH BUTTERFLIES ARE DYING AND BEE COLONIES ARE COLLAPSING ACROSS THE UNITED STATES.
KEEP OUT! CONSTRUCTION ZONE
HERE AT EARHART, A GROUP OF GIRLS CALLED THE GEEKY FAB 5 HAS ADOPTED THIS GARDEN, AND THEY WANT TO KNOW: WHO WANTS TO BULLDOZE THIS LOT?
I ASKED QUESTIONS AT CITY HALL TODAY. WHAT I HAVE LEARNED IS THAT A DEVELOPER WANTS TO BUILD A CONVENIENCE STORE AND GAS STATION, CALLED "LICKIES AND CHEWIES."
CITY HALL
THE DEVELOPER'S IDENTITY IS A SECRET RIGHT NOW, BUT WORD IS THE BULLDOZERS WILL START ROLLING IN ABOUT 2 TO 3 WEEKS.
WYXZ
THAT'S WHEN THE CATERPILLARS WILL BECOME BUTTERFLIES. WE CAN'T LET THIS HAPPEN!
WHAT MEANIES WOULD WRECK A GARDEN? WE NEED TO FIND OUT WHO THOUGHT UP THIS DUMB IDEA!
NOW, NOW, LUCY. MAYBE THEY DON'T KNOW THAT THOSE BUTTERFLIES ARE THERE. ALTHOUGH I BET THEY KNOW NOW...

"TO STAY HOPEFUL UNTIL WE HEARD FROM SUZY, WE HUNG OUT AT A.J.'S HOUSE. SINCE MOVING TO NORMAL, OUR FAVORITE SATURDAYS ARE SPENT HANGING WITH A.J. AND HER DAD WHO LOVE FIXING UP WHAT SOFIA THINKS LOOKS LIKE A LADYBUG."

DO YOU THINK LADYBUGS HAVE EYELASHES, LUCY?

WELL, THEY DO NOW!

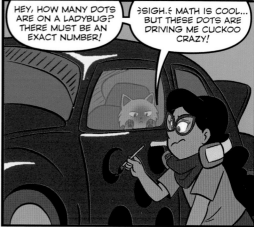

HEY, HOW MANY DOTS ARE ON A LADYBUG? THERE MUST BE AN EXACT NUMBER!

≷SIGH.≷ MATH IS COOL... BUT THESE DOTS ARE DRIVING ME CUCKOO CRAZY!

A.J., YOUR ROBOTIC SKATEBOARD IS GENIUS. ALBERT LOVES IT!

OH, LOOK. FOOD TO GO. MAY I HAVE A CATERPILLAR VALUE MEAL WITH A SIDE OF FRIES?

THIS IS JUST *TOO CUTE!*

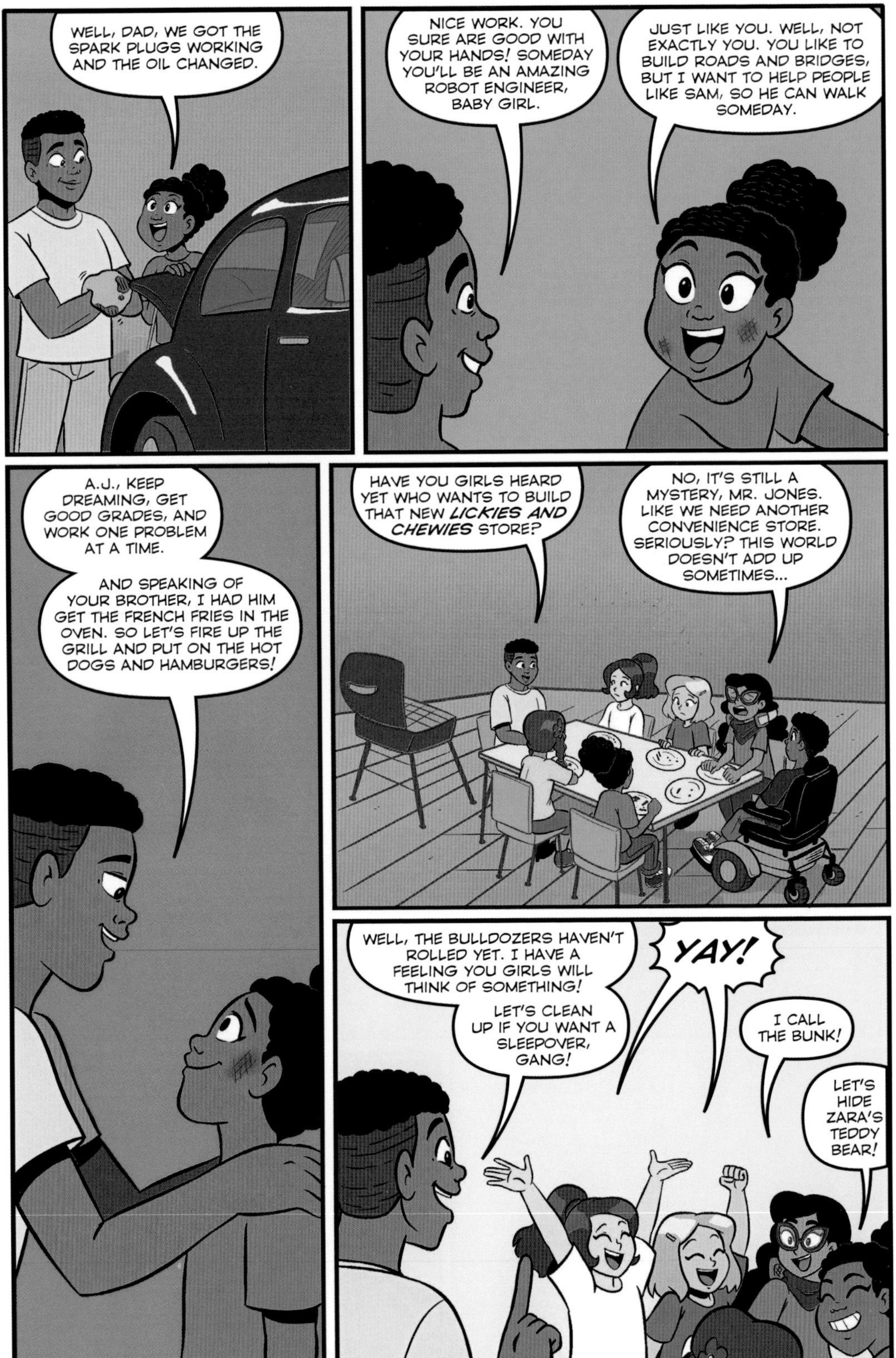
WELL, DAD, WE GOT THE SPARK PLUGS WORKING AND THE OIL CHANGED.
NICE WORK. YOU SURE ARE GOOD WITH YOUR HANDS! SOMEDAY YOU'LL BE AN AMAZING ROBOT ENGINEER, BABY GIRL.
JUST LIKE YOU. WELL, NOT EXACTLY YOU. YOU LIKE TO BUILD ROADS AND BRIDGES, BUT I WANT TO HELP PEOPLE LIKE SAM, SO HE CAN WALK SOMEDAY.
A.J., KEEP DREAMING, GET GOOD GRADES, AND WORK ONE PROBLEM AT A TIME.
AND SPEAKING OF YOUR BROTHER, I HAD HIM GET THE FRENCH FRIES IN THE OVEN. SO LET'S FIRE UP THE GRILL AND PUT ON THE HOT DOGS AND HAMBURGERS!
HAVE YOU GIRLS HEARD YET WHO WANTS TO BUILD THAT NEW *LICKIES AND CHEWIES* STORE?
NO, IT'S STILL A MYSTERY, MR. JONES. LIKE WE NEED ANOTHER CONVENIENCE STORE. SERIOUSLY? THIS WORLD DOESN'T ADD UP SOMETIMES...
WELL, THE BULLDOZERS HAVEN'T ROLLED YET. I HAVE A FEELING YOU GIRLS WILL THINK OF SOMETHING!
LET'S CLEAN UP IF YOU WANT A SLEEPOVER, GANG!
YAY!
I CALL THE BUNK!
LET'S HIDE ZARA'S TEDDY BEAR!

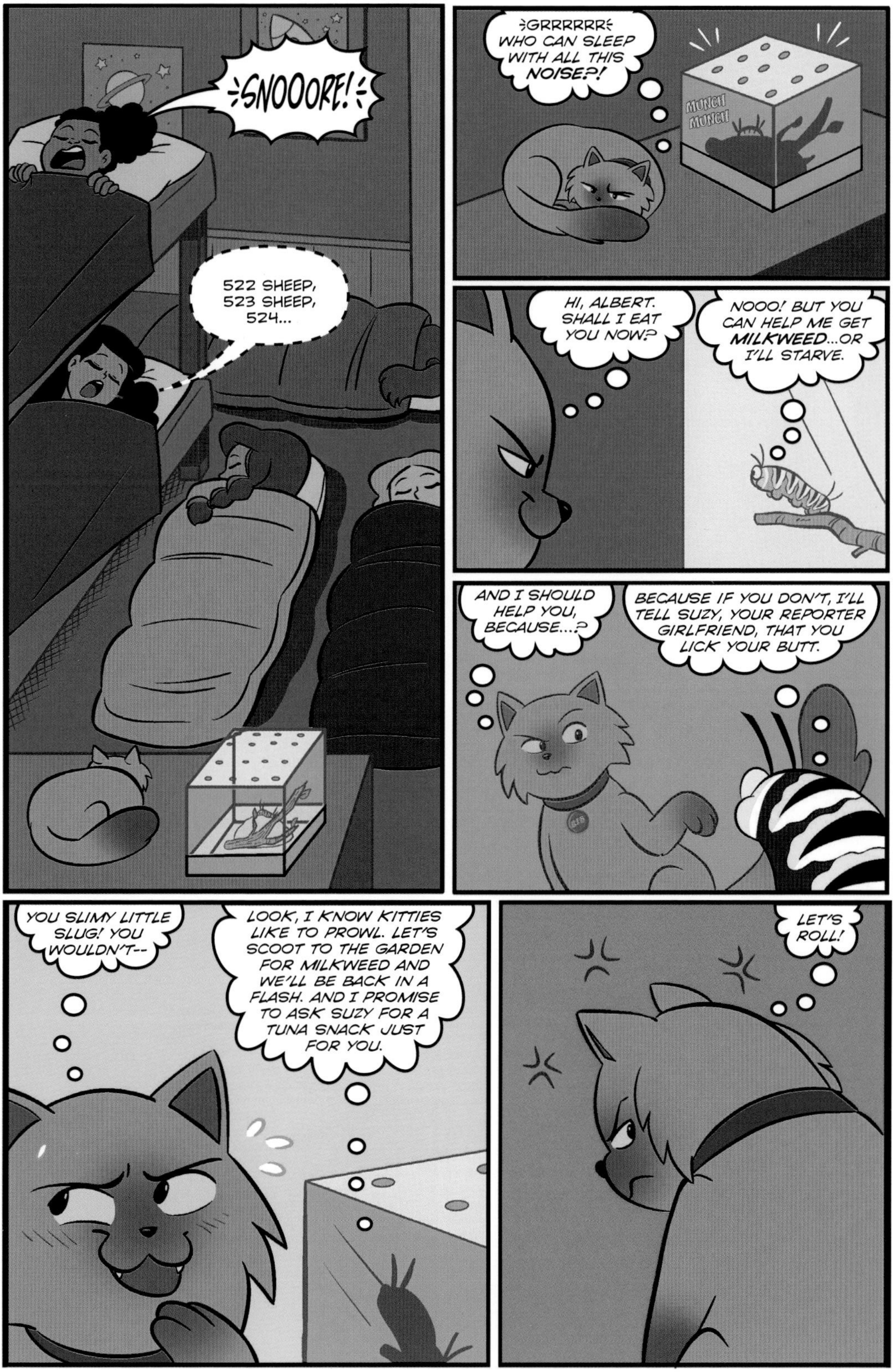
SNOOORE!
522 SHEEP, 523 SHEEP, 524...
GRRRRRR WHO CAN SLEEP WITH ALL THIS NOISE?!
MUNCH MUNCH
HI, ALBERT. SHALL I EAT YOU NOW?
NOOO! BUT YOU CAN HELP ME GET MILKWEED...OR I'LL STARVE.
AND I SHOULD HELP YOU, BECAUSE...?
BECAUSE IF YOU DON'T, I'LL TELL SUZY, YOUR REPORTER GIRLFRIEND, THAT YOU LICK YOUR BUTT.
YOU SLIMY LITTLE SLUG! YOU WOULDN'T--
LOOK, I KNOW KITTIES LIKE TO PROWL. LET'S SCOOT TO THE GARDEN FOR MILKWEED AND WE'LL BE BACK IN A FLASH. AND I PROMISE TO ASK SUZY FOR A TUNA SNACK JUST FOR YOU.
LET'S ROLL!

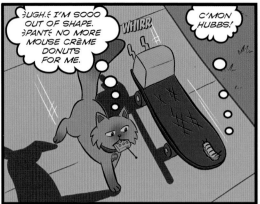

‡UGH.‡ I'M SOOO OUT OF SHAPE. ‡PANT‡ NO MORE MOUSE CRÈME DONUTS FOR ME.

C'MON HUBBS!

WHIRR

‡PANT!‡ ‡PANT!‡ THIS IS WHAT I GET FOR SKIPPING WORKOUTS!

ALMOST THERE. MUST. HAVE. MILKWEED. SO HUNGRY. STOMACH IS GROWLING!

YOU'LL BE IN MY FURRY STOMACH IF YOU DON'T SHUT YOUR MINI-MOUTH!

THANK THE TUNA GODS, FINALLY THE GARDEN!

WHOA. HOLD UP! I SEE A LIGHT! SOMEONE IS SNEAKING AROUND! ‡SHHH!‡

KEEP OUT! CONSTRUCTION ZONE

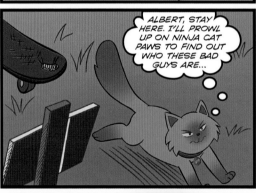

ALBERT, STAY HERE. I'LL PROWL UP ON NINJA CAT PAWS TO FIND OUT WHO THESE BAD GUYS ARE...

I KNOW YOU! ‡HISSSSSSSSSS!‡

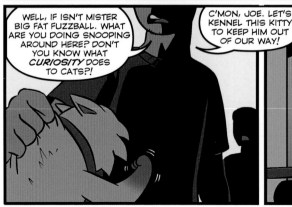

WELL, IF ISN'T MISTER BIG FAT FUZZBALL. WHAT ARE YOU DOING SNOOPING AROUND HERE? DON'T YOU KNOW WHAT CURIOSITY DOES TO CATS?!

C'MON, JOE. LET'S KENNEL THIS KITTY TO KEEP HIM OUT OF OUR WAY!

DON'T WORRY, HUBBLE. I GOTCHA. WELL, AS SOON AS I HAVE SOME MILKWEED, THAT IS!

30

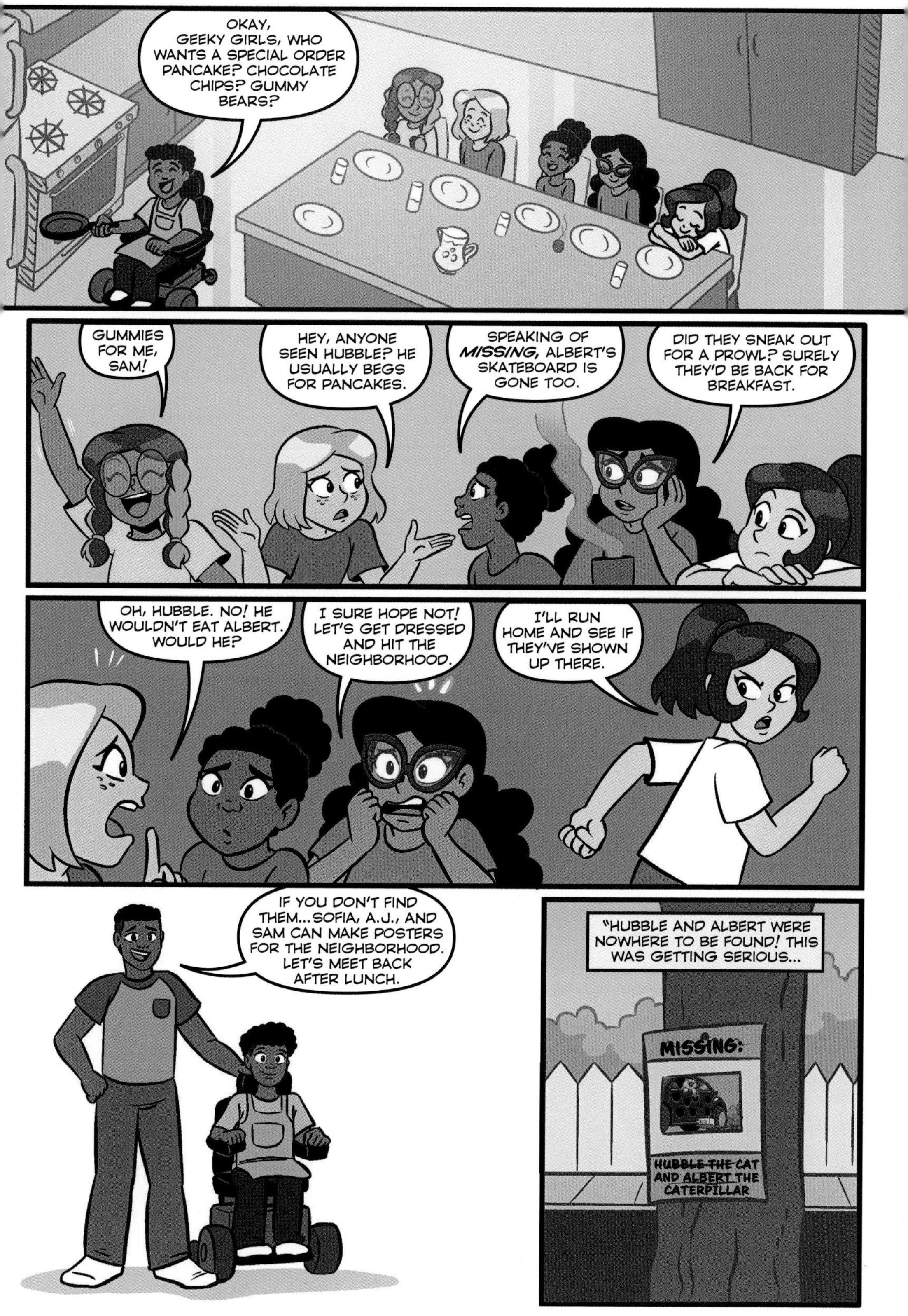
OKAY, GEEKY GIRLS, WHO WANTS A SPECIAL ORDER PANCAKE? CHOCOLATE CHIPS? GUMMY BEARS?
GUMMIES FOR ME, SAM!
HEY, ANYONE SEEN HUBBLE? HE USUALLY BEGS FOR PANCAKES.
SPEAKING OF *MISSING*, ALBERT'S SKATEBOARD IS GONE TOO.
DID THEY SNEAK OUT FOR A PROWL? SURELY THEY'D BE BACK FOR BREAKFAST.
OH, HUBBLE. NO! HE WOULDN'T EAT ALBERT. WOULD HE?
I SURE HOPE NOT! LET'S GET DRESSED AND HIT THE NEIGHBORHOOD.
I'LL RUN HOME AND SEE IF THEY'VE SHOWN UP THERE.
IF YOU DON'T FIND THEM...SOFIA, A.J., AND SAM CAN MAKE POSTERS FOR THE NEIGHBORHOOD. LET'S MEET BACK AFTER LUNCH.
"HUBBLE AND ALBERT WERE NOWHERE TO BE FOUND! THIS WAS GETTING SERIOUS...
MISSING:
HUBBLE THE CAT AND ALBERT THE CATERPILLAR

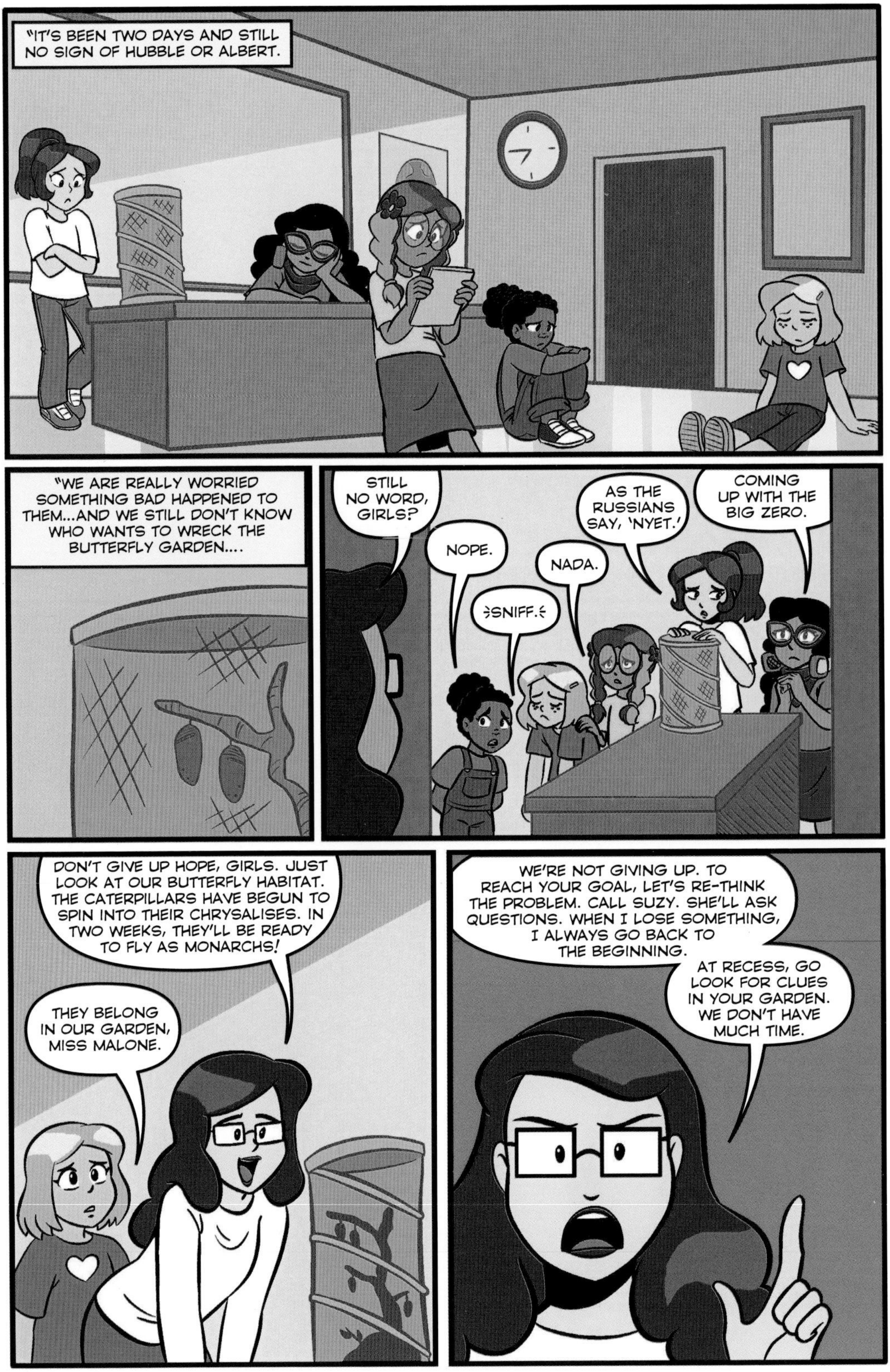
"IT'S BEEN TWO DAYS AND STILL NO SIGN OF HUBBLE OR ALBERT.
"WE ARE REALLY WORRIED SOMETHING BAD HAPPENED TO THEM...AND WE STILL DON'T KNOW WHO WANTS TO WRECK THE BUTTERFLY GARDEN....
STILL NO WORD, GIRLS?
NOPE.
:SNIFF.:
NADA.
AS THE RUSSIANS SAY, 'NYET.'
COMING UP WITH THE BIG ZERO.
DON'T GIVE UP HOPE, GIRLS. JUST LOOK AT OUR BUTTERFLY HABITAT. THE CATERPILLARS HAVE BEGUN TO SPIN INTO THEIR CHRYSALISES. IN TWO WEEKS, THEY'LL BE READY TO FLY AS MONARCHS!
THEY BELONG IN OUR GARDEN, MISS MALONE.
WE'RE NOT GIVING UP. TO REACH YOUR GOAL, LET'S RE-THINK THE PROBLEM. CALL SUZY. SHE'LL ASK QUESTIONS. WHEN I LOSE SOMETHING, I ALWAYS GO BACK TO THE BEGINNING.
AT RECESS, GO LOOK FOR CLUES IN YOUR GARDEN. WE DON'T HAVE MUCH TIME.

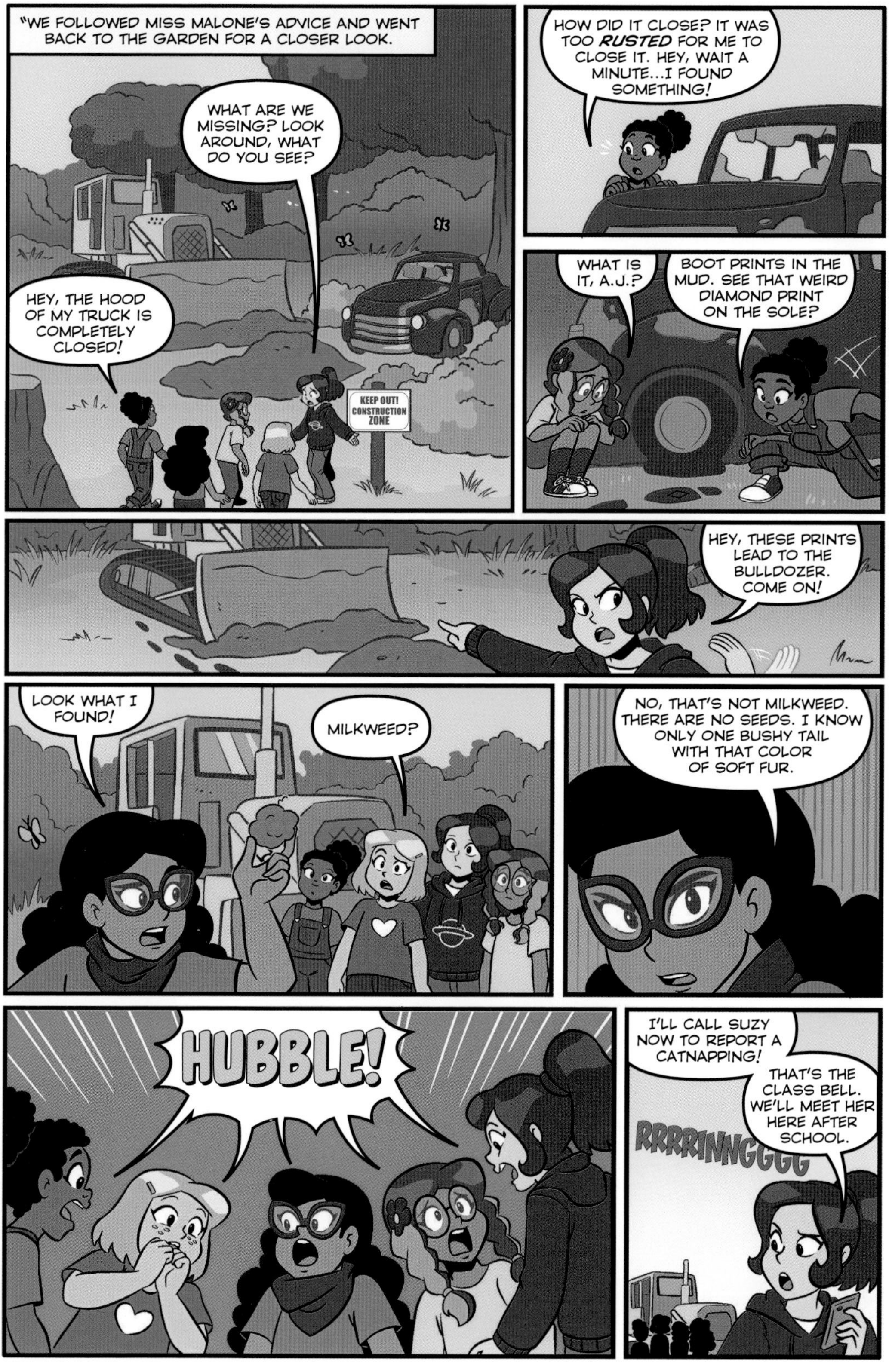
"WE FOLLOWED MISS MALONE'S ADVICE AND WENT BACK TO THE GARDEN FOR A CLOSER LOOK.
WHAT ARE WE MISSING? LOOK AROUND, WHAT DO YOU SEE?
HEY, THE HOOD OF MY TRUCK IS COMPLETELY CLOSED!
KEEP OUT! CONSTRUCTION ZONE
HOW DID IT CLOSE? IT WAS TOO RUSTED FOR ME TO CLOSE IT. HEY, WAIT A MINUTE...I FOUND SOMETHING!
WHAT IS IT, A.J.?
BOOT PRINTS IN THE MUD. SEE THAT WEIRD DIAMOND PRINT ON THE SOLE?
HEY, THESE PRINTS LEAD TO THE BULLDOZER. COME ON!
LOOK WHAT I FOUND!
MILKWEED?
NO, THAT'S NOT MILKWEED. THERE ARE NO SEEDS. I KNOW ONLY ONE BUSHY TAIL WITH THAT COLOR OF SOFT FUR.
HUBBLE!
I'LL CALL SUZY NOW TO REPORT A CATNAPPING!
RRRRINNGGGG
THAT'S THE CLASS BELL. WE'LL MEET HER HERE AFTER SCHOOL.

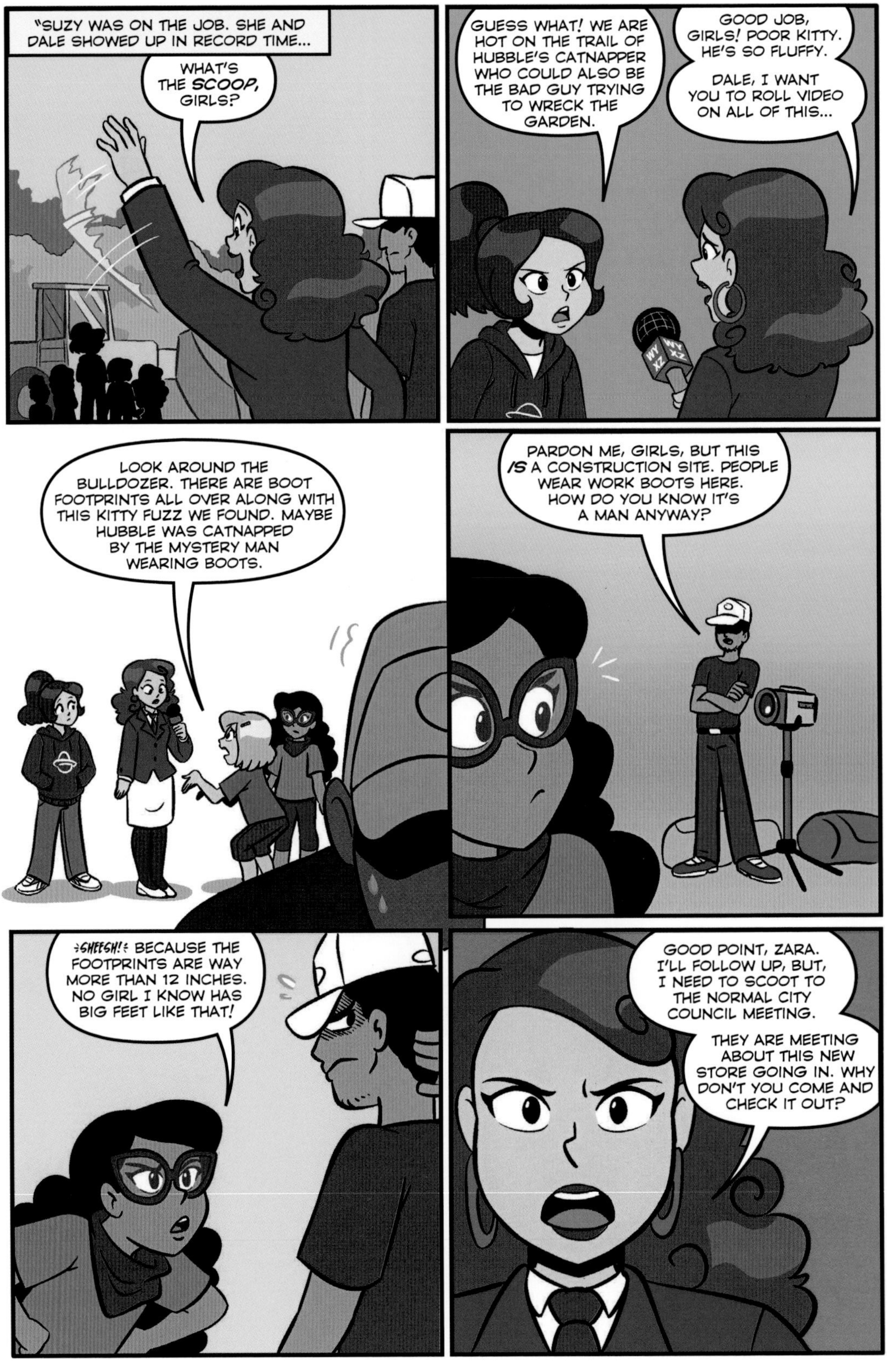
"SUZY WAS ON THE JOB. SHE AND DALE SHOWED UP IN RECORD TIME...
WHAT'S THE SCOOP, GIRLS?
GUESS WHAT! WE ARE HOT ON THE TRAIL OF HUBBLE'S CATNAPPER WHO COULD ALSO BE THE BAD GUY TRYING TO WRECK THE GARDEN.
GOOD JOB, GIRLS! POOR KITTY. HE'S SO FLUFFY.
DALE, I WANT YOU TO ROLL VIDEO ON ALL OF THIS...
WY XZ
LOOK AROUND THE BULLDOZER. THERE ARE BOOT FOOTPRINTS ALL OVER ALONG WITH THIS KITTY FUZZ WE FOUND. MAYBE HUBBLE WAS CATNAPPED BY THE MYSTERY MAN WEARING BOOTS.
PARDON ME, GIRLS, BUT THIS IS A CONSTRUCTION SITE. PEOPLE WEAR WORK BOOTS HERE. HOW DO YOU KNOW IT'S A MAN ANYWAY?
SHEESH! BECAUSE THE FOOTPRINTS ARE WAY MORE THAN 12 INCHES. NO GIRL I KNOW HAS BIG FEET LIKE THAT!
GOOD POINT, ZARA. I'LL FOLLOW UP, BUT, I NEED TO SCOOT TO THE NORMAL CITY COUNCIL MEETING.
THEY ARE MEETING ABOUT THIS NEW STORE GOING IN. WHY DON'T YOU COME AND CHECK IT OUT?

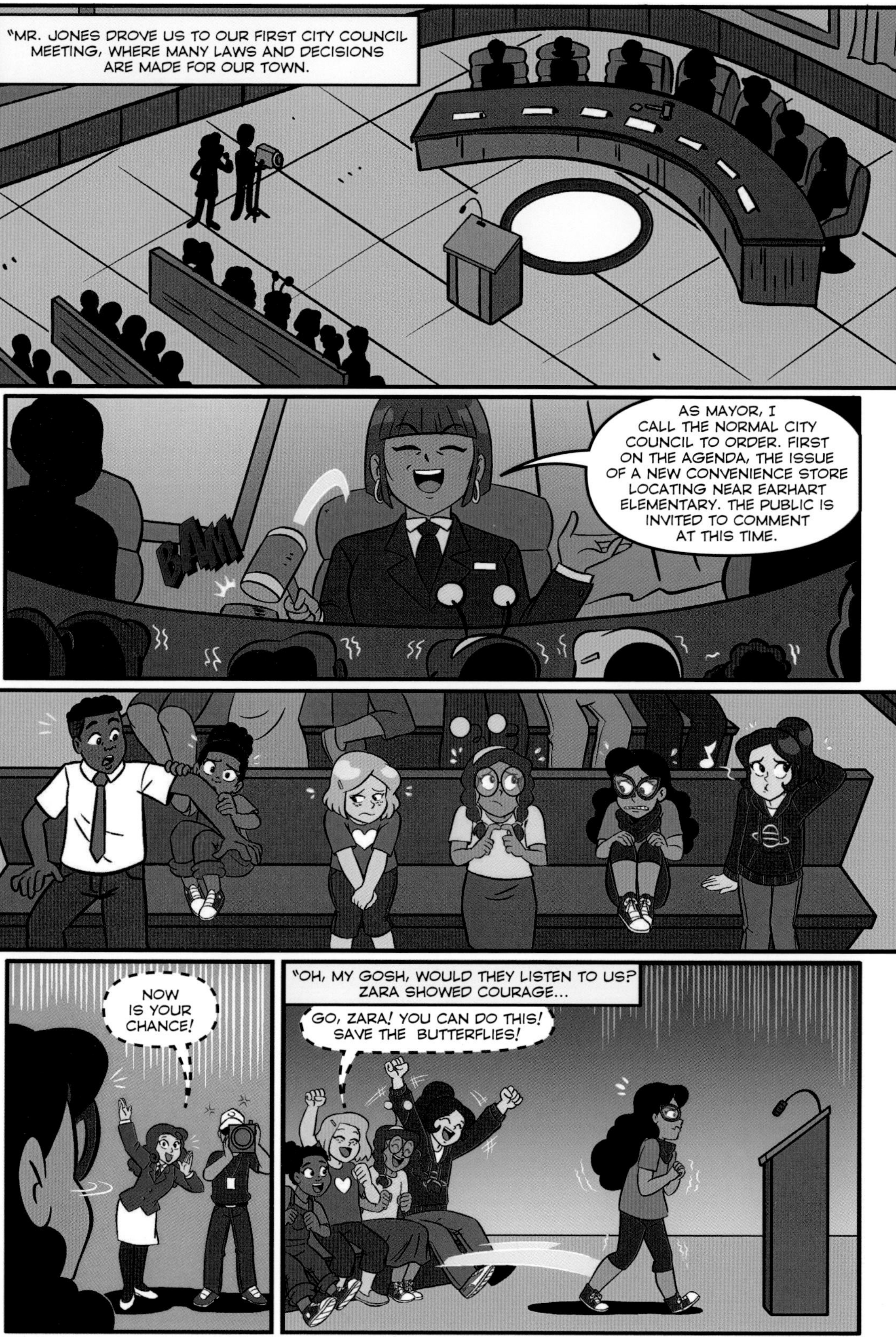
"MR. JONES DROVE US TO OUR FIRST CITY COUNCIL MEETING, WHERE MANY LAWS AND DECISIONS ARE MADE FOR OUR TOWN.
AS MAYOR, I CALL THE NORMAL CITY COUNCIL TO ORDER. FIRST ON THE AGENDA, THE ISSUE OF A NEW CONVENIENCE STORE LOCATING NEAR EARHART ELEMENTARY. THE PUBLIC IS INVITED TO COMMENT AT THIS TIME.
BAM
NOW IS YOUR CHANCE!
"OH, MY GOSH, WOULD THEY LISTEN TO US? ZARA SHOWED COURAGE...
GO, ZARA! YOU CAN DO THIS! SAVE THE BUTTERFLIES!

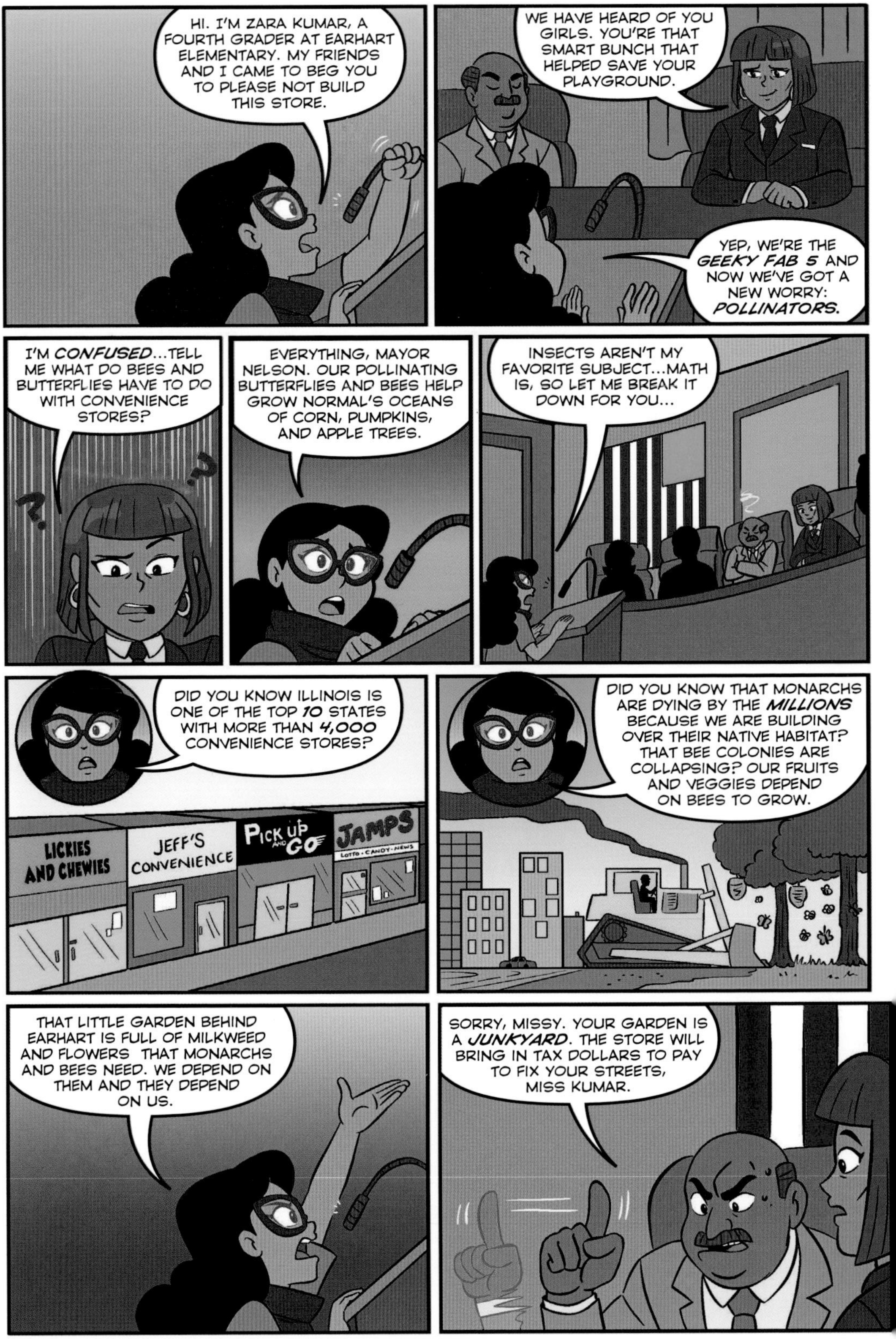
HI. I'M ZARA KUMAR, A FOURTH GRADER AT EARHART ELEMENTARY. MY FRIENDS AND I CAME TO BEG YOU TO PLEASE NOT BUILD THIS STORE.
WE HAVE HEARD OF YOU GIRLS. YOU'RE THAT SMART BUNCH THAT HELPED SAVE YOUR PLAYGROUND.
YEP, WE'RE THE GEEKY FAB 5 AND NOW WE'VE GOT A NEW WORRY: POLLINATORS.
I'M CONFUSED...TELL ME WHAT DO BEES AND BUTTERFLIES HAVE TO DO WITH CONVENIENCE STORES?
EVERYTHING, MAYOR NELSON. OUR POLLINATING BUTTERFLIES AND BEES HELP GROW NORMAL'S OCEANS OF CORN, PUMPKINS, AND APPLE TREES.
INSECTS AREN'T MY FAVORITE SUBJECT...MATH IS, SO LET ME BREAK IT DOWN FOR YOU...
DID YOU KNOW ILLINOIS IS ONE OF THE TOP 10 STATES WITH MORE THAN 4,000 CONVENIENCE STORES?
LICKIES AND CHEWIES
JEFF'S CONVENIENCE
PICK UP AND GO
JAMPS
LOTTO · CANDY · NEWS
DID YOU KNOW THAT MONARCHS ARE DYING BY THE MILLIONS BECAUSE WE ARE BUILDING OVER THEIR NATIVE HABITAT? THAT BEE COLONIES ARE COLLAPSING? OUR FRUITS AND VEGGIES DEPEND ON BEES TO GROW.
THAT LITTLE GARDEN BEHIND EARHART IS FULL OF MILKWEED AND FLOWERS THAT MONARCHS AND BEES NEED. WE DEPEND ON THEM AND THEY DEPEND ON US.
SORRY, MISSY. YOUR GARDEN IS A JUNKYARD. THE STORE WILL BRING IN TAX DOLLARS TO PAY TO FIX YOUR STREETS, MISS KUMAR.

EXCUSE ME, SIR, BUT DO WE REALLY NEED ANOTHER CONVENIENCE STORE PAVING OVER WILDFLOWERS NEXT TO OUR SCHOOL? WE NEED TO PROTECT OUR AWESOME WORLD AND OUR FOOD!

THANK YOU, ZARA, FOR YOUR VERY THOUGHTFUL PRESENTATION. WE'LL THINK ABOUT YOUR REQUEST WHEN WE VOTE ON THIS PROJECT NEXT WEEK. WE DON'T OWN THE LAND, BUT ITS OWNER HAS ASKED US TO APPROVE THE PLANS.

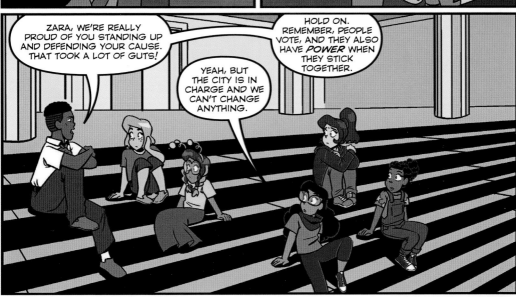

ZARA, WE'RE REALLY PROUD OF YOU STANDING UP AND DEFENDING YOUR CAUSE. THAT TOOK A LOT OF GUTS!

YEAH, BUT THE CITY IS IN CHARGE AND WE CAN'T CHANGE ANYTHING.

HOLD ON. REMEMBER, PEOPLE VOTE, AND THEY ALSO HAVE *POWER* WHEN THEY STICK TOGETHER.

WE NEED TO FIND OUT WHO OWNS THAT LAND. OUR MONARCHS ARE IN THEIR CHRYSALIS STAGE AT SCHOOL AND TIME IS RUNNING OUT.

YOU CAN'T START A MOVEMENT ON AN EMPTY STOMACH. WHO WANTS ICE CREAM? I'M BUYING!

I CALL A COOKIE DOUGH SHAKE!

MINT CHOCOLATE CHIP!

CHOCOLATE SWIRL!

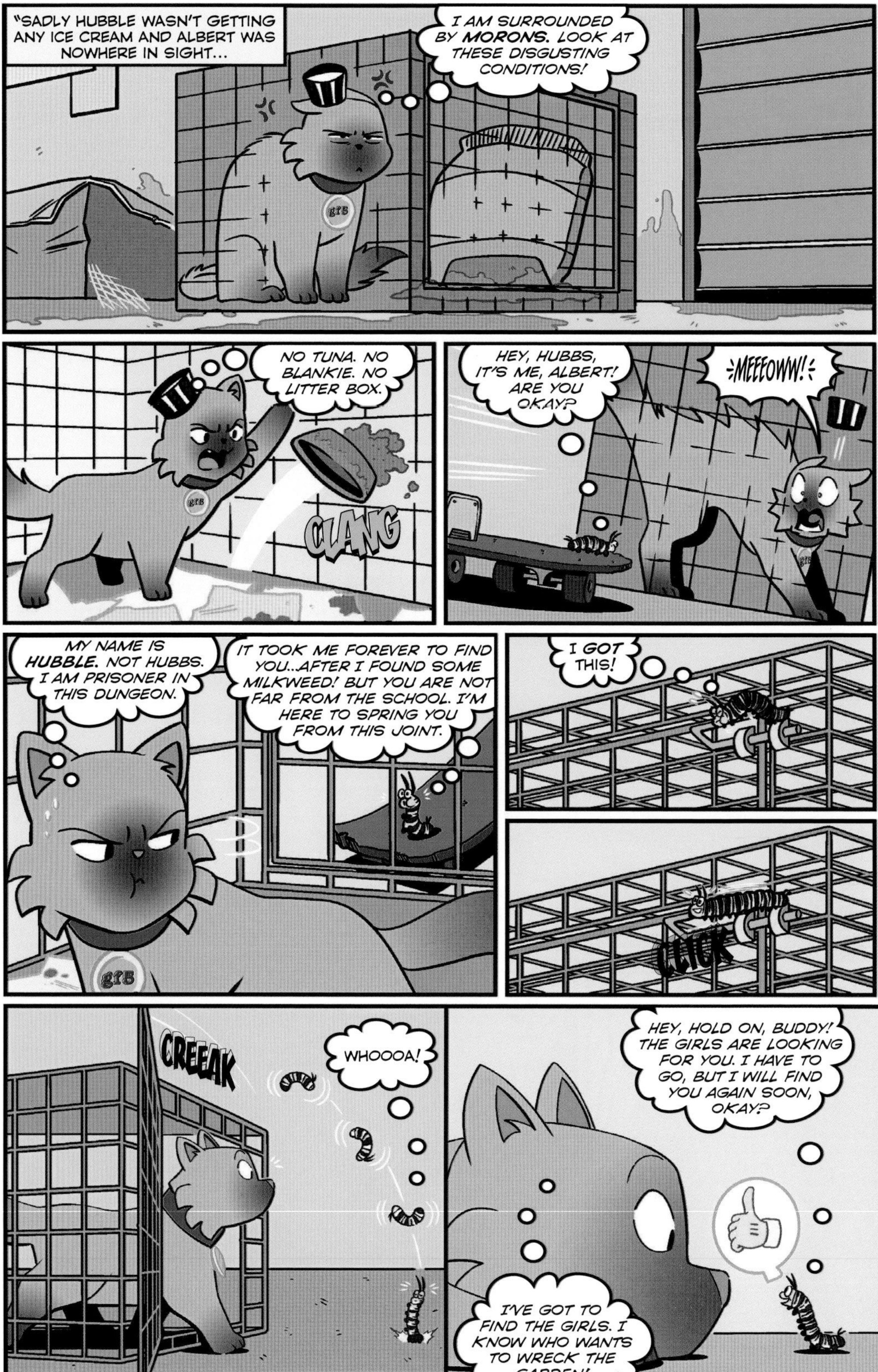
"SADLY HUBBLE WASN'T GETTING ANY ICE CREAM AND ALBERT WAS NOWHERE IN SIGHT...
I AM SURROUNDED BY MORONS. LOOK AT THESE DISGUSTING CONDITIONS!
NO TUNA. NO BLANKIE. NO LITTER BOX.
CLANG
HEY, HUBBS, IT'S ME, ALBERT! ARE YOU OKAY?
MEEEOWW!
MY NAME IS HUBBLE. NOT HUBBS. I AM PRISONER IN THIS DUNGEON.
IT TOOK ME FOREVER TO FIND YOU...AFTER I FOUND SOME MILKWEED! BUT YOU ARE NOT FAR FROM THE SCHOOL. I'M HERE TO SPRING YOU FROM THIS JOINT.
I GOT THIS!
CLICK
CREEAK
WHOOOA!
HEY, HOLD ON, BUDDY! THE GIRLS ARE LOOKING FOR YOU. I HAVE TO GO, BUT I WILL FIND YOU AGAIN SOON, OKAY?
I'VE GOT TO FIND THE GIRLS. I KNOW WHO WANTS TO WRECK THE GARDEN!

CHAPTER SIX: BAD GUYS

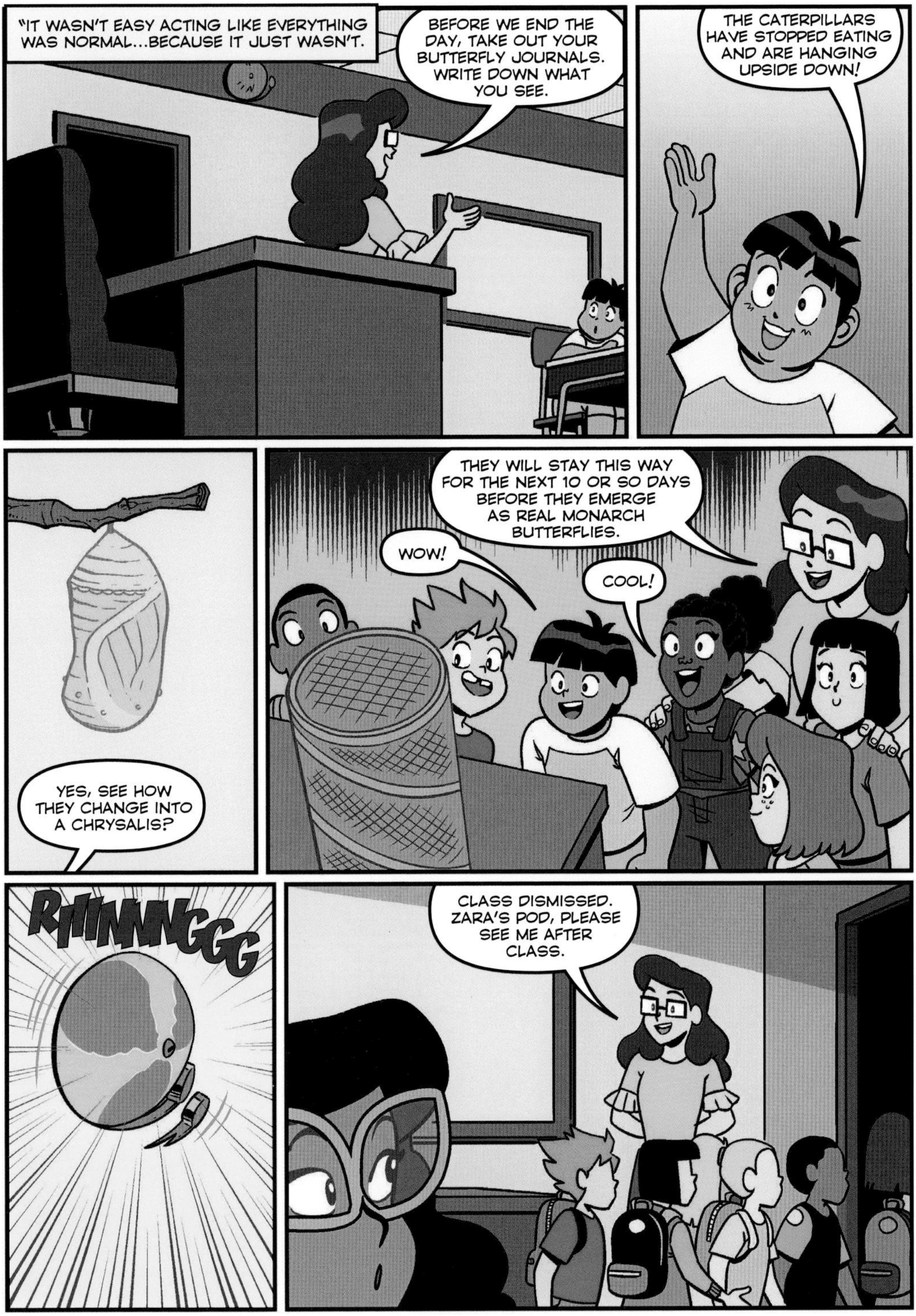

"IT WASN'T EASY ACTING LIKE EVERYTHING WAS NORMAL...BECAUSE IT JUST WASN'T.
BEFORE WE END THE DAY, TAKE OUT YOUR BUTTERFLY JOURNALS. WRITE DOWN WHAT YOU SEE.
THE CATERPILLARS HAVE STOPPED EATING AND ARE HANGING UPSIDE DOWN!
YES, SEE HOW THEY CHANGE INTO A CHRYSALIS?
THEY WILL STAY THIS WAY FOR THE NEXT 10 OR SO DAYS BEFORE THEY EMERGE AS REAL MONARCH BUTTERFLIES.
WOW!
COOL!
RIIINNNGGG
CLASS DISMISSED. ZARA'S POD, PLEASE SEE ME AFTER CLASS.

ANY LUCK WITH THE GARDEN MYSTERY?

NO, EVERYTHING IS *AWFUL!* HUBBLE IS STILL MISSING. THE CITY COUNCIL IS VOTING ON THE PROJECT TONIGHT...AND NO ONE CARES THAT WE'RE HURTING OUR PLANET.

YOU KNOW, LUCY, YOU AREN'T THE FIRST WOMAN WHO TRIED TO WARN OTHERS ABOUT HURTING WILDLIFE. HAVE YOU EVER HEARD OF *RACHEL CARSON?*

NO. WHO WAS SHE?

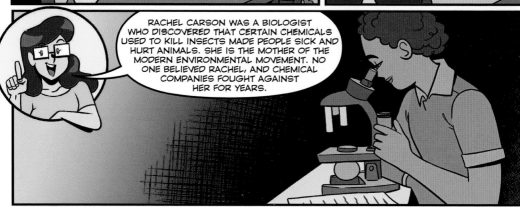

RACHEL CARSON WAS A BIOLOGIST WHO DISCOVERED THAT CERTAIN CHEMICALS USED TO KILL INSECTS MADE PEOPLE SICK AND HURT ANIMALS. SHE IS THE MOTHER OF THE MODERN ENVIRONMENTAL MOVEMENT. NO ONE BELIEVED RACHEL, AND CHEMICAL COMPANIES FOUGHT AGAINST HER FOR YEARS.

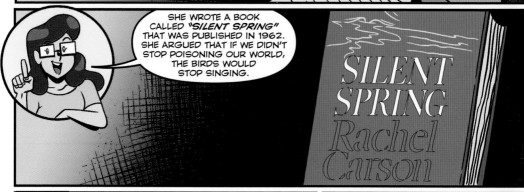

SHE WROTE A BOOK CALLED *"SILENT SPRING"* THAT WAS PUBLISHED IN 1962. SHE ARGUED THAT IF WE DIDN'T STOP POISONING OUR WORLD, THE BIRDS WOULD STOP SINGING.

SILENT SPRING
Rachel Carson

IMAGINE... NO BIRDS.

NO BUTTERFLIES.

NO BEES.

NO. NO. *NO!* WE FIGHT THIS!

ZARA'S RIGHT. IT'S UP TO THE *GEEKY FAB 5.* LET'S MEET TONIGHT ON TOP OF THE SCHOOL ROOF. MARINA IS SETTING UP HER TELESCOPE TO SEE SATURN. WE'LL MAKE BATTLE PLANS.

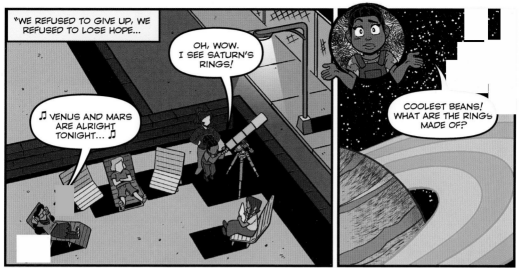

"WE REFUSED TO GIVE UP, WE REFUSED TO LOSE HOPE...

OH, WOW. I SEE SATURN'S RINGS!

♫ VENUS AND MARS ARE ALRIGHT TONIGHT... ♫

COOLEST BEANS! WHAT ARE THE RINGS MADE OF?

TINY PIECES OF ROCKS, ICE, AND WATER. SATURN IS MORE THAN 800 MILLION MILES FROM EARTH! ZARA, CHECK IT OUT!

800,000,000 -- THAT'S EIGHT ZEROS. AWESOME!

IT WOULD TAKE MANY YEARS JUST TO FLY THERE. I'M GOING TO MARS FIRST...MUCH CLOSER!

⸰SIGH.⸰ I PREFER EARTH, THANK YOU. EXCEPT FOR THE FACT WE ARE DESTROYING IT.

⸰SHHH!⸰ DID YOU ALL HEAR SOMETHING?

MEOW!

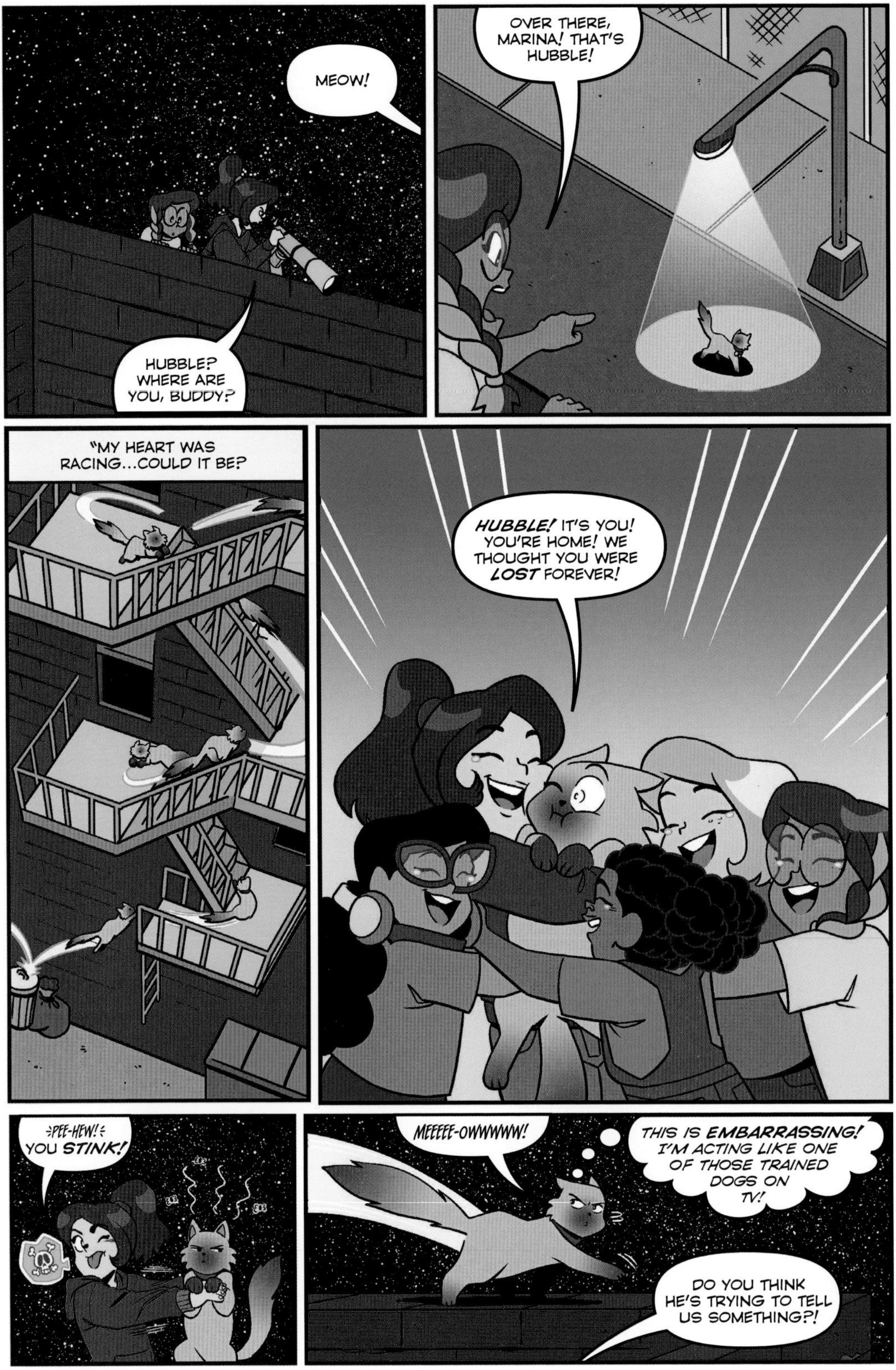
MEOW!
HUBBLE? WHERE ARE YOU, BUDDY?
OVER THERE, MARINA! THAT'S HUBBLE!
"MY HEART WAS RACING...COULD IT BE?
HUBBLE! IT'S YOU! YOU'RE HOME! WE THOUGHT YOU WERE LOST FOREVER!
PEE-HEW! YOU STINK!
MEEEEE-OWWWWW!
THIS IS EMBARRASSING! I'M ACTING LIKE ONE OF THOSE TRAINED DOGS ON TV!
DO YOU THINK HE'S TRYING TO TELL US SOMETHING?!

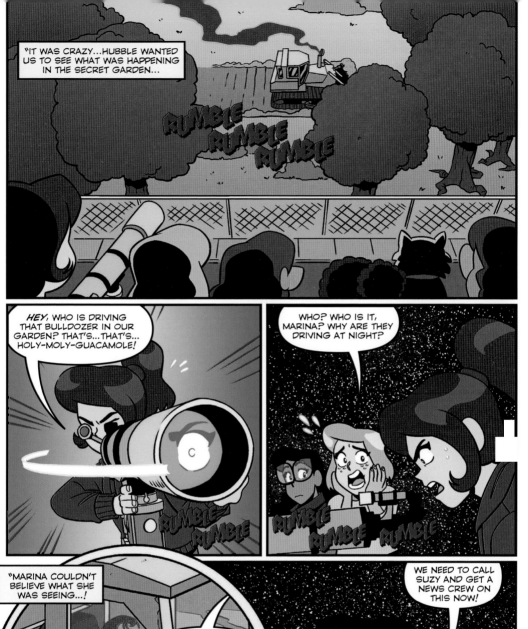

"IT WAS CRAZY...HUBBLE WANTED US TO SEE WHAT WAS HAPPENING IN THE SECRET GARDEN...

RUMBLE RUMBLE RUMBLE

HEY, WHO IS DRIVING THAT BULLDOZER IN OUR GARDEN? THAT'S...THAT'S... HOLY-MOLY-GUACAMOLE!

RUMBLE RUMBLE

WHO? WHO IS IT, MARINA? WHY ARE THEY DRIVING AT NIGHT?

RUMBLE RUMBLE RUMBLE

"MARINA COULDN'T BELIEVE WHAT SHE WAS SEEING...!

IT'S—IT'S DALE... THE CAMERAMAN.

WE NEED TO CALL SUZY AND GET A NEWS CREW ON THIS NOW!

RUMBLE RUMBLE RUMBLE

RUMBLE RUMBLE

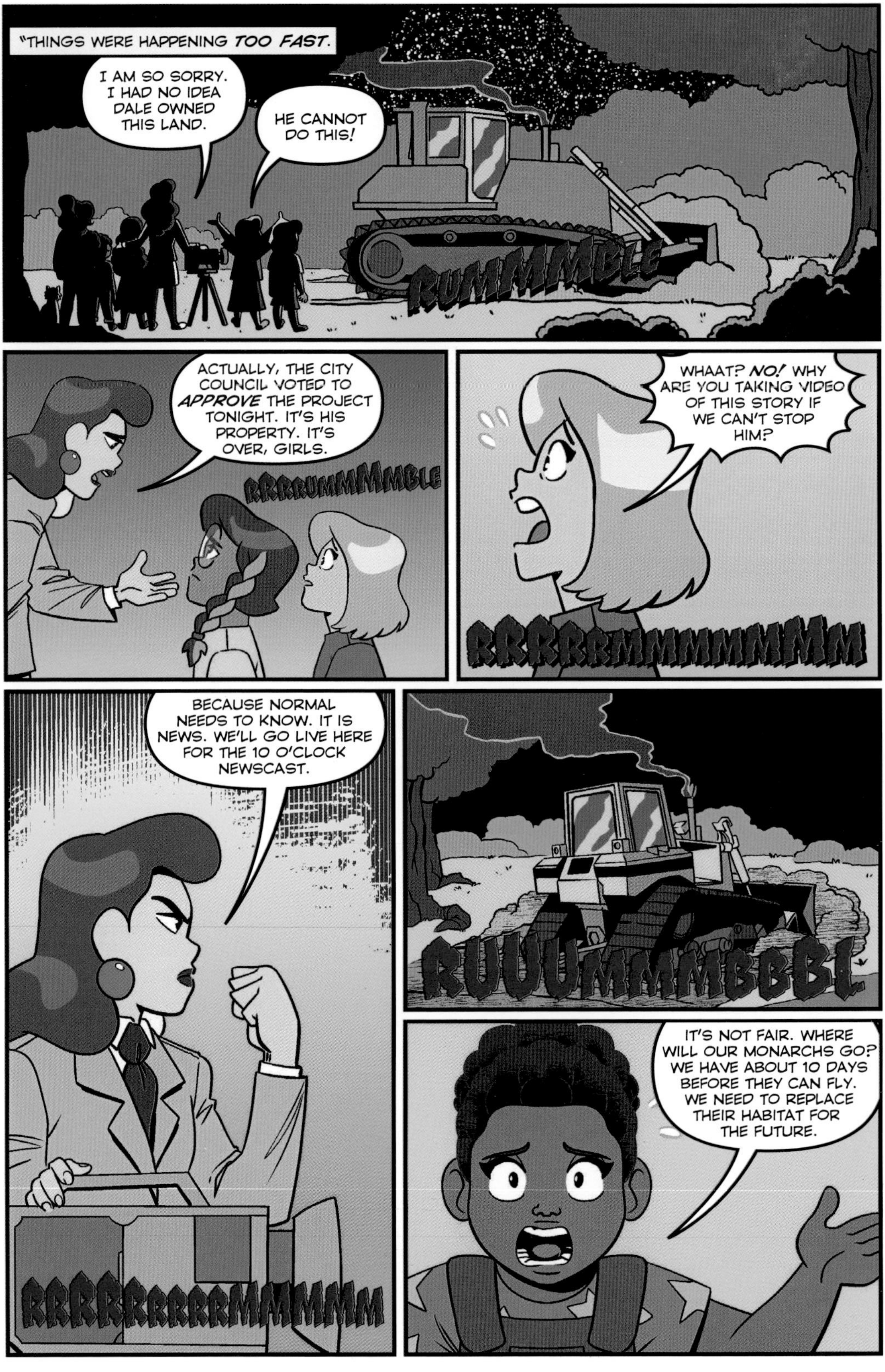
"THINGS WERE HAPPENING *TOO FAST*.
I AM SO SORRY. I HAD NO IDEA DALE OWNED THIS LAND.
HE CANNOT DO THIS!
RUMMMBLE
ACTUALLY, THE CITY COUNCIL VOTED TO *APPROVE* THE PROJECT TONIGHT. IT'S HIS PROPERTY. IT'S OVER, GIRLS.
RRRRUMMMMMBLE
WHAAT? *NO!* WHY ARE YOU TAKING VIDEO OF THIS STORY IF WE CAN'T STOP HIM?
RRRRRMMMMMMMMM
BECAUSE NORMAL NEEDS TO KNOW. IT IS NEWS. WE'LL GO LIVE HERE FOR THE 10 O'CLOCK NEWSCAST.
RRRRrrrrrRMMMMMM
RUUUMMMMBBBL
IT'S NOT FAIR. WHERE WILL OUR MONARCHS GO? WE HAVE ABOUT 10 DAYS BEFORE THEY CAN FLY. WE NEED TO REPLACE THEIR HABITAT FOR THE FUTURE.

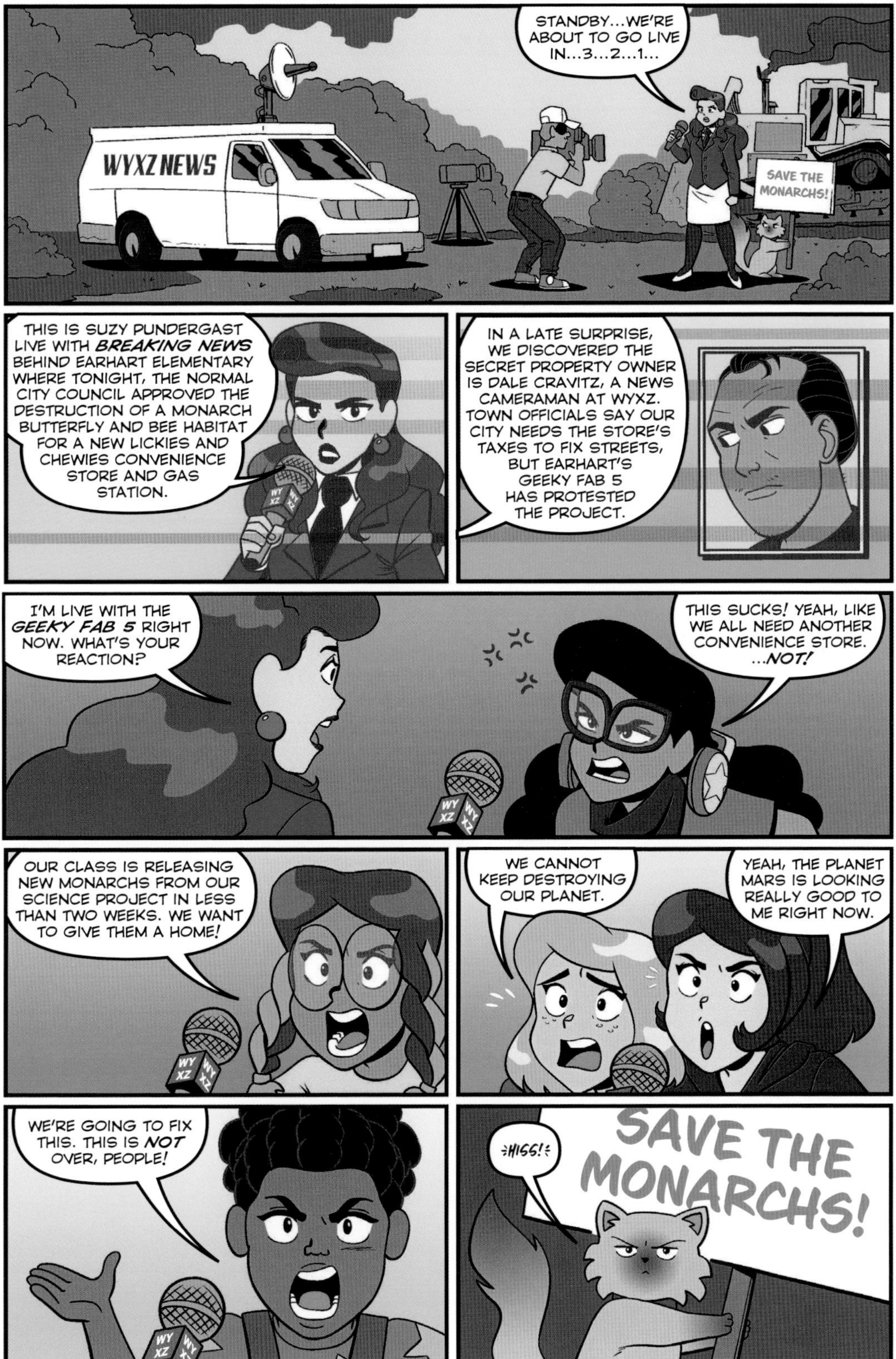
STANDBY...WE'RE ABOUT TO GO LIVE IN...3...2...1...
WYXZ NEWS
SAVE THE MONARCHS!
THIS IS SUZY PUNDERGAST LIVE WITH BREAKING NEWS BEHIND EARHART ELEMENTARY WHERE TONIGHT, THE NORMAL CITY COUNCIL APPROVED THE DESTRUCTION OF A MONARCH BUTTERFLY AND BEE HABITAT FOR A NEW LICKIES AND CHEWIES CONVENIENCE STORE AND GAS STATION.
IN A LATE SURPRISE, WE DISCOVERED THE SECRET PROPERTY OWNER IS DALE CRAVITZ, A NEWS CAMERAMAN AT WYXZ. TOWN OFFICIALS SAY OUR CITY NEEDS THE STORE'S TAXES TO FIX STREETS, BUT EARHART'S GEEKY FAB 5 HAS PROTESTED THE PROJECT.
I'M LIVE WITH THE GEEKY FAB 5 RIGHT NOW. WHAT'S YOUR REACTION?
THIS SUCKS! YEAH, LIKE WE ALL NEED ANOTHER CONVENIENCE STORE. ...NOT!
OUR CLASS IS RELEASING NEW MONARCHS FROM OUR SCIENCE PROJECT IN LESS THAN TWO WEEKS. WE WANT TO GIVE THEM A HOME!
WE CANNOT KEEP DESTROYING OUR PLANET.
YEAH, THE PLANET MARS IS LOOKING REALLY GOOD TO ME RIGHT NOW.
WE'RE GOING TO FIX THIS. THIS IS NOT OVER, PEOPLE!
HISS!
SAVE THE MONARCHS!

CHAPTER SEVEN: PEOPLE POWER

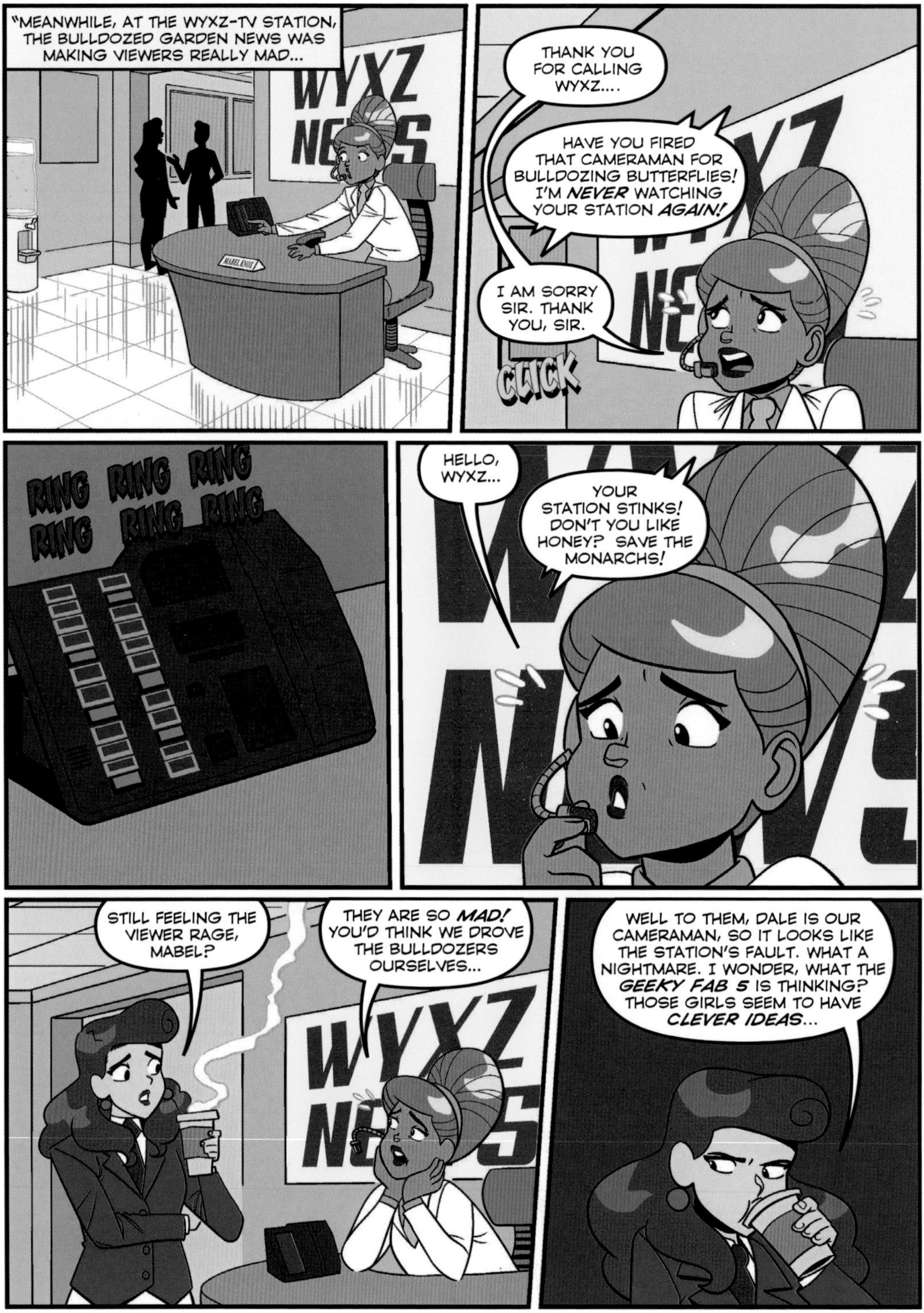

"MEANWHILE, AT THE WYXZ-TV STATION, THE BULLDOZED GARDEN NEWS WAS MAKING VIEWERS REALLY MAD...
WYXZ NEWS
MABEL KNOX
THANK YOU FOR CALLING WYXZ....
HAVE YOU FIRED THAT CAMERAMAN FOR BULLDOZING BUTTERFLIES! I'M *NEVER* WATCHING YOUR STATION *AGAIN!*
I AM SORRY SIR. THANK YOU, SIR.
CLICK
RING RING RING RING RING RING
HELLO, WYXZ...
YOUR STATION STINKS! DON'T YOU LIKE HONEY? SAVE THE MONARCHS!
STILL FEELING THE VIEWER RAGE, MABEL?
THEY ARE SO *MAD!* YOU'D THINK WE DROVE THE BULLDOZERS OURSELVES...
WYXZ NEWS
WELL TO THEM, DALE IS OUR CAMERAMAN, SO IT LOOKS LIKE THE STATION'S FAULT. WHAT A NIGHTMARE. I WONDER, WHAT THE *GEEKY FAB 5* IS THINKING? THOSE GIRLS SEEM TO HAVE *CLEVER IDEAS*...

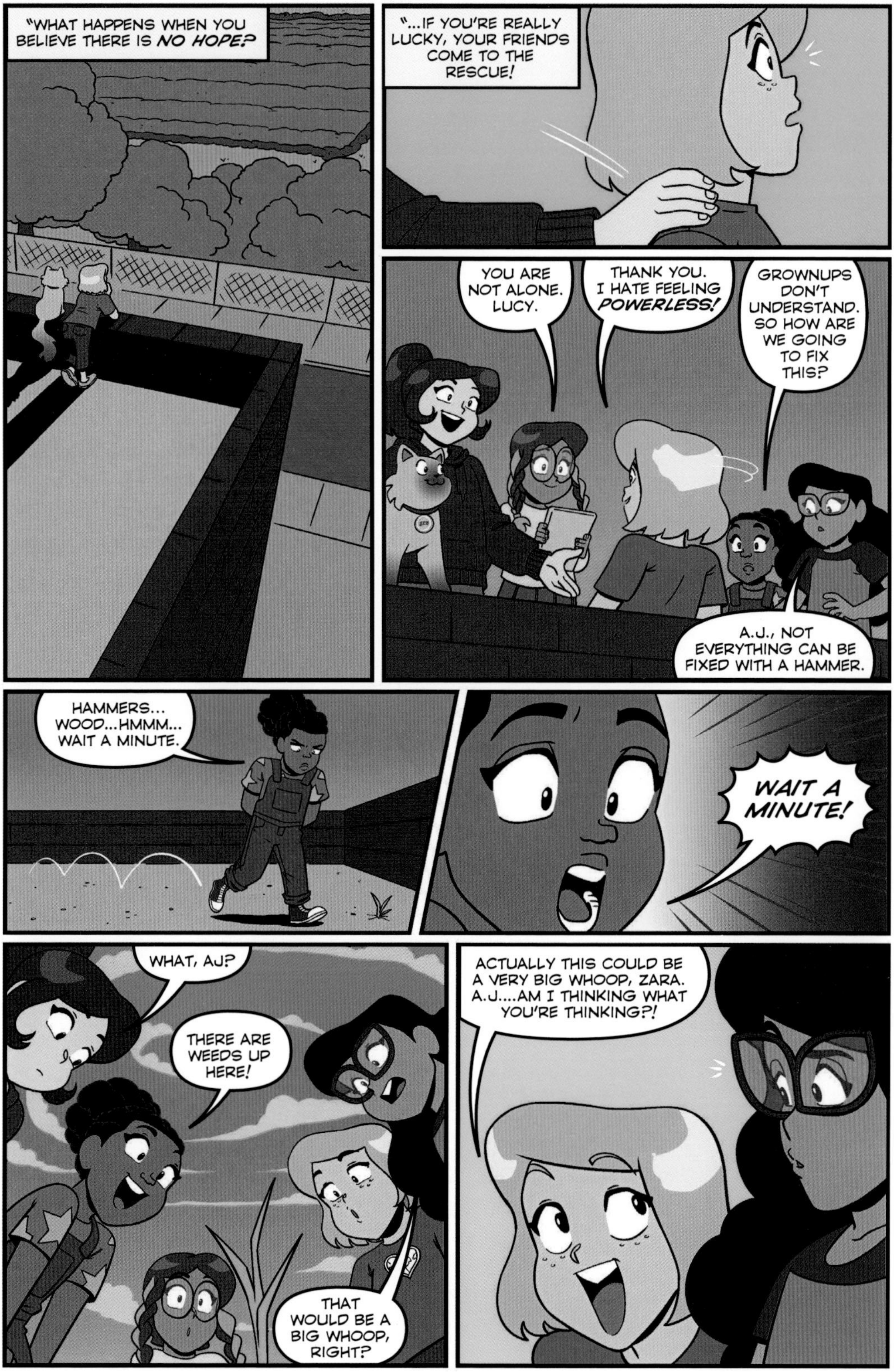
"WHAT HAPPENS WHEN YOU BELIEVE THERE IS NO HOPE?
"...IF YOU'RE REALLY LUCKY, YOUR FRIENDS COME TO THE RESCUE!
YOU ARE NOT ALONE. LUCY.
THANK YOU. I HATE FEELING POWERLESS!
GROWNUPS DON'T UNDERSTAND. SO HOW ARE WE GOING TO FIX THIS?
A.J., NOT EVERYTHING CAN BE FIXED WITH A HAMMER.
HAMMERS... WOOD...HMMM... WAIT A MINUTE.
WAIT A MINUTE!
WHAT, AJ?
THERE ARE WEEDS UP HERE!
THAT WOULD BE A BIG WHOOP, RIGHT?
ACTUALLY THIS COULD BE A VERY BIG WHOOP, ZARA. A.J....AM I THINKING WHAT YOU'RE THINKING?!

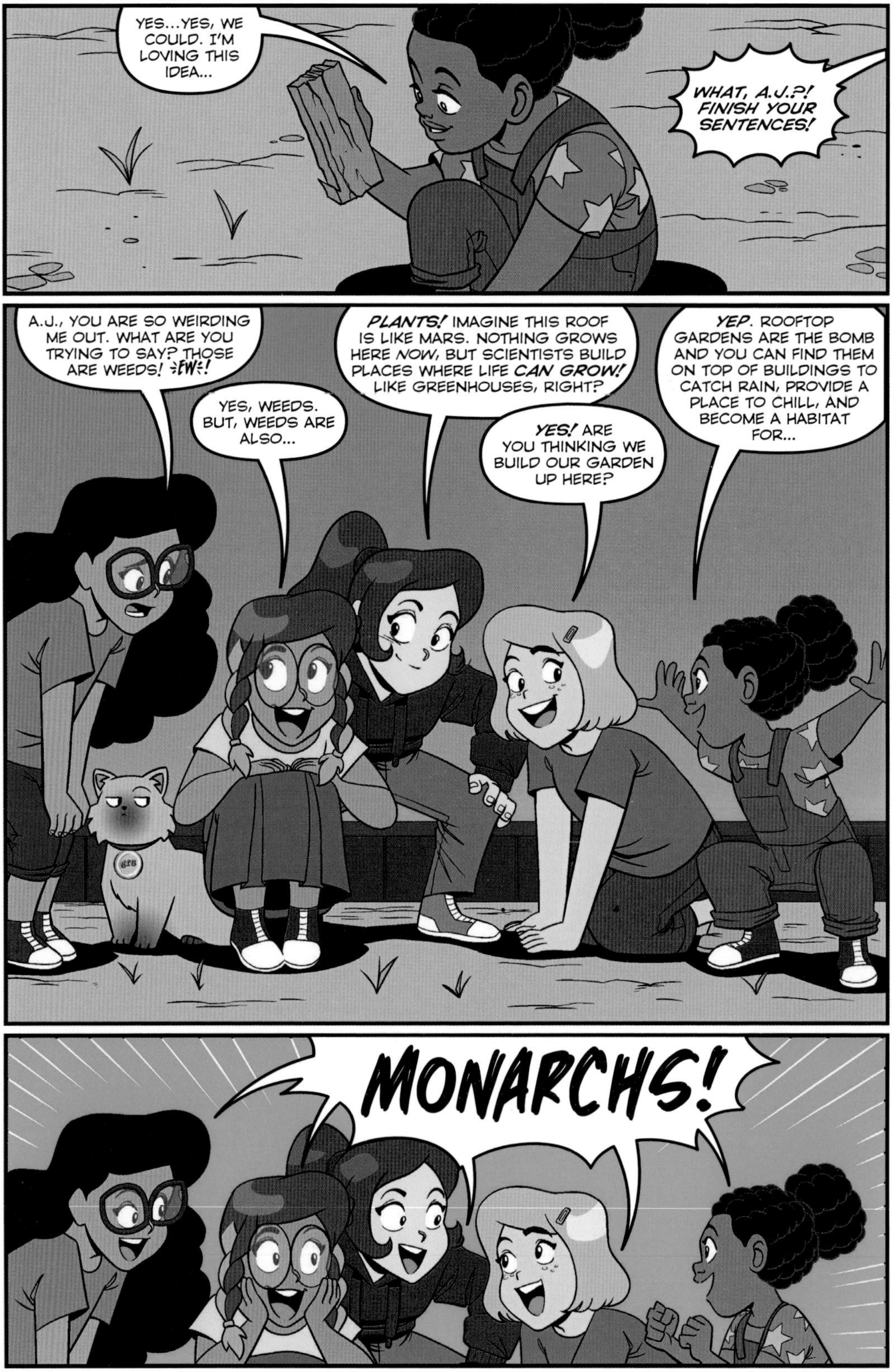
YES...YES, WE COULD. I'M LOVING THIS IDEA...
WHAT, A.J.?! FINISH YOUR SENTENCES!
A.J., YOU ARE SO WEIRDING ME OUT. WHAT ARE YOU TRYING TO SAY? THOSE ARE WEEDS! EW!
YES, WEEDS. BUT, WEEDS ARE ALSO...
PLANTS! IMAGINE THIS ROOF IS LIKE MARS. NOTHING GROWS HERE NOW, BUT SCIENTISTS BUILD PLACES WHERE LIFE CAN GROW! LIKE GREENHOUSES, RIGHT?
YES! ARE YOU THINKING WE BUILD OUR GARDEN UP HERE?
YEP. ROOFTOP GARDENS ARE THE BOMB AND YOU CAN FIND THEM ON TOP OF BUILDINGS TO CATCH RAIN, PROVIDE A PLACE TO CHILL, AND BECOME A HABITAT FOR...
MONARCHS!

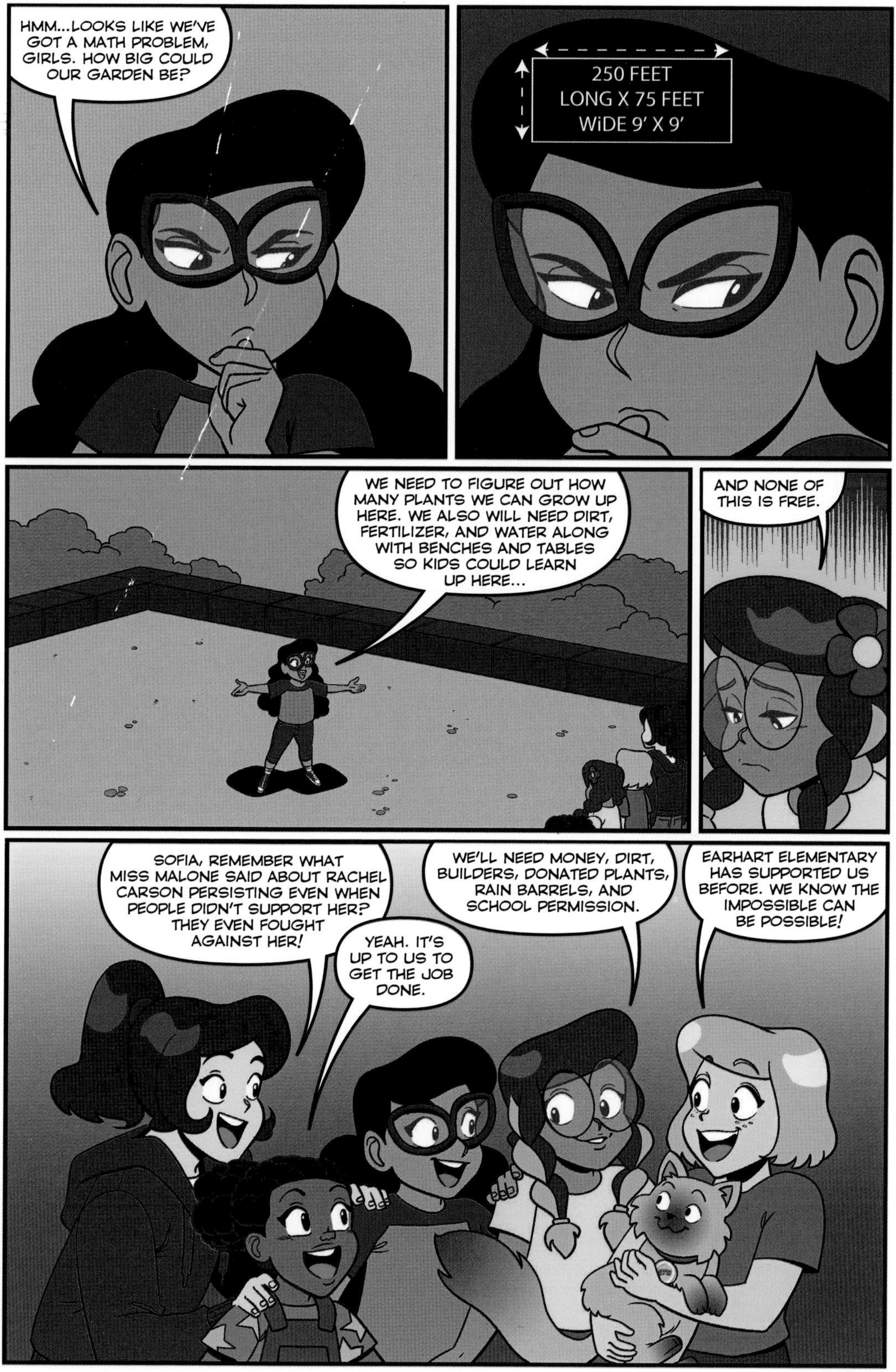
HMM...LOOKS LIKE WE'VE GOT A MATH PROBLEM, GIRLS. HOW BIG COULD OUR GARDEN BE?
250 FEET LONG X 75 FEET WiDE 9' X 9'
WE NEED TO FIGURE OUT HOW MANY PLANTS WE CAN GROW UP HERE. WE ALSO WILL NEED DIRT, FERTILIZER, AND WATER ALONG WITH BENCHES AND TABLES SO KIDS COULD LEARN UP HERE...
AND NONE OF THIS IS FREE.
SOFIA, REMEMBER WHAT MISS MALONE SAID ABOUT RACHEL CARSON PERSISTING EVEN WHEN PEOPLE DIDN'T SUPPORT HER? THEY EVEN FOUGHT AGAINST HER!
YEAH. IT'S UP TO US TO GET THE JOB DONE.
WE'LL NEED MONEY, DIRT, BUILDERS, DONATED PLANTS, RAIN BARRELS, AND SCHOOL PERMISSION.
EARHART ELEMENTARY HAS SUPPORTED US BEFORE. WE KNOW THE IMPOSSIBLE CAN BE POSSIBLE!

CHAPTER EIGHT: BEE BOLD. BEE BRAVE. BEE FIERCE.

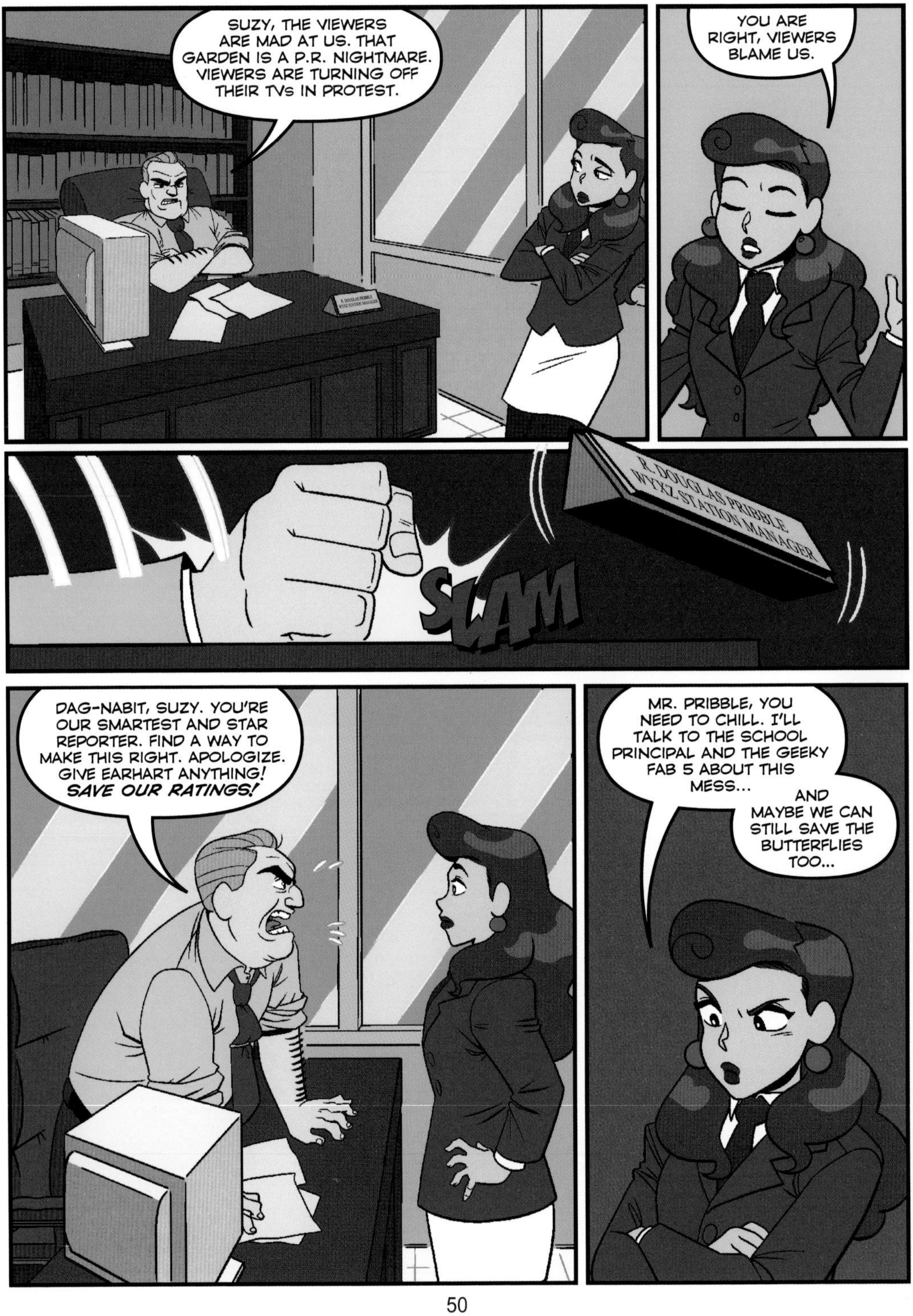
SUZY, THE VIEWERS ARE MAD AT US. THAT GARDEN IS A P.R. NIGHTMARE. VIEWERS ARE TURNING OFF THEIR TVs IN PROTEST.
YOU ARE RIGHT, VIEWERS BLAME US.
R. DOUGLAS PRIBBLE WYXZ STATION MANAGER
SLAM
DAG-NABIT, SUZY. YOU'RE OUR SMARTEST AND STAR REPORTER. FIND A WAY TO MAKE THIS RIGHT. APOLOGIZE. GIVE EARHART ANYTHING! *SAVE OUR RATINGS!*
MR. PRIBBLE, YOU NEED TO CHILL. I'LL TALK TO THE SCHOOL PRINCIPAL AND THE GEEKY FAB 5 ABOUT THIS MESS...
AND MAYBE WE CAN STILL SAVE THE BUTTERFLIES TOO...

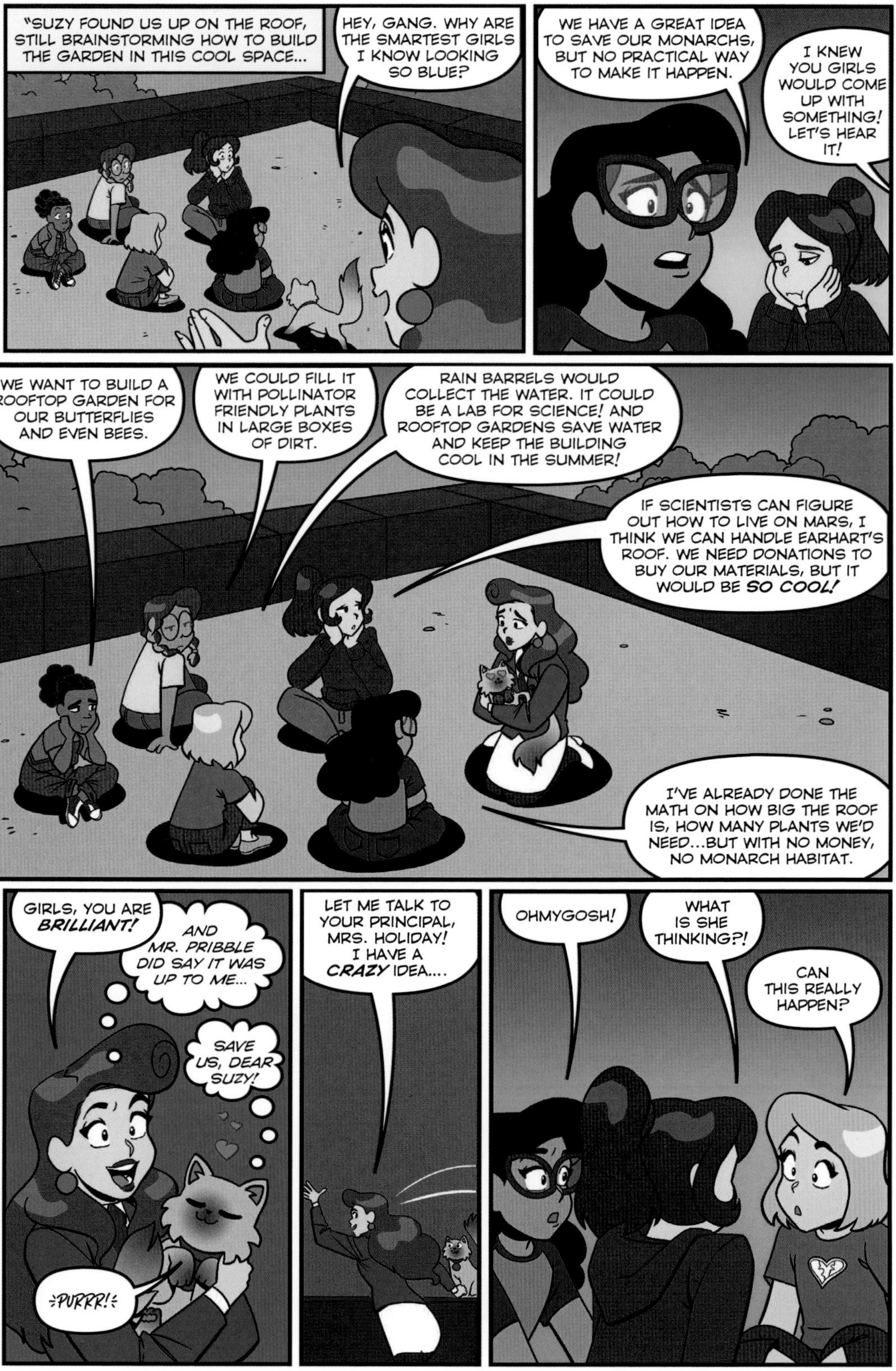
"SUZY FOUND US UP ON THE ROOF, STILL BRAINSTORMING HOW TO BUILD THE GARDEN IN THIS COOL SPACE...
HEY, GANG. WHY ARE THE SMARTEST GIRLS I KNOW LOOKING SO BLUE?
WE HAVE A GREAT IDEA TO SAVE OUR MONARCHS, BUT NO PRACTICAL WAY TO MAKE IT HAPPEN.
I KNEW YOU GIRLS WOULD COME UP WITH SOMETHING! LET'S HEAR IT!
WE WANT TO BUILD A ROOFTOP GARDEN FOR OUR BUTTERFLIES AND EVEN BEES.
WE COULD FILL IT WITH POLLINATOR FRIENDLY PLANTS IN LARGE BOXES OF DIRT.
RAIN BARRELS WOULD COLLECT THE WATER. IT COULD BE A LAB FOR SCIENCE! AND ROOFTOP GARDENS SAVE WATER AND KEEP THE BUILDING COOL IN THE SUMMER!
IF SCIENTISTS CAN FIGURE OUT HOW TO LIVE ON MARS, I THINK WE CAN HANDLE EARHART'S ROOF. WE NEED DONATIONS TO BUY OUR MATERIALS, BUT IT WOULD BE ***SO COOL!***
I'VE ALREADY DONE THE MATH ON HOW BIG THE ROOF IS, HOW MANY PLANTS WE'D NEED...BUT WITH NO MONEY, NO MONARCH HABITAT.
GIRLS, YOU ARE ***BRILLIANT!***
AND MR. PRIBBLE DID SAY IT WAS UP TO ME...
SAVE US, DEAR SUZY!
PURRR!
LET ME TALK TO YOUR PRINCIPAL, MRS. HOLIDAY! I HAVE A ***CRAZY*** IDEA....
OHMYGOSH!
WHAT IS SHE THINKING?!
CAN THIS REALLY HAPPEN?

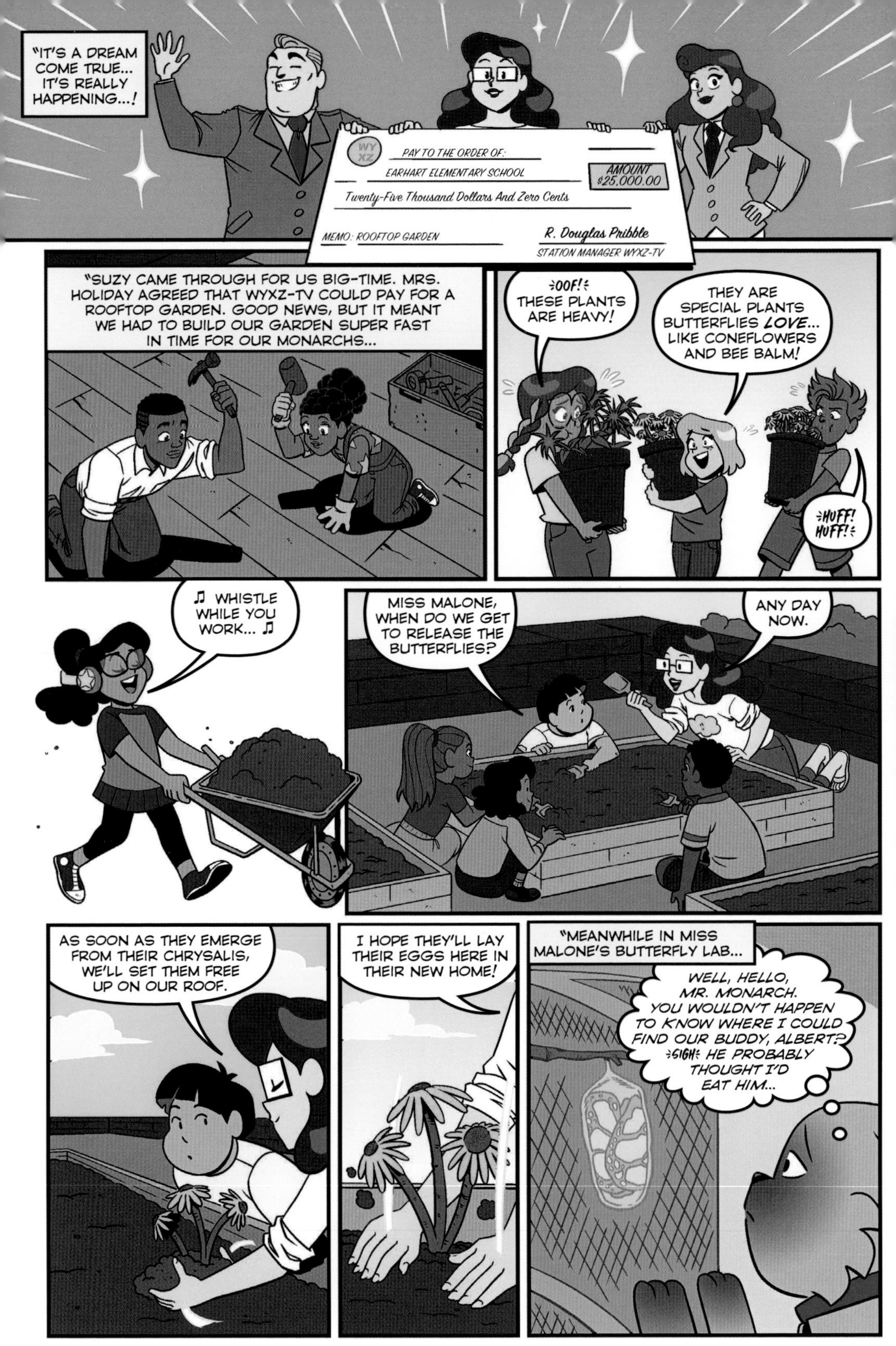
"IT'S A DREAM COME TRUE... IT'S REALLY HAPPENING...!
WY XZ
PAY TO THE ORDER OF:
EARHART ELEMENTARY SCHOOL
AMOUNT $25,000.00
Twenty-Five Thousand Dollars And Zero Cents
MEMO: ROOFTOP GARDEN
R. Douglas Pribble
STATION MANAGER WYXZ-TV
"SUZY CAME THROUGH FOR US BIG-TIME. MRS. HOLIDAY AGREED THAT WYXZ-TV COULD PAY FOR A ROOFTOP GARDEN. GOOD NEWS, BUT IT MEANT WE HAD TO BUILD OUR GARDEN SUPER FAST IN TIME FOR OUR MONARCHS...
OOF! THESE PLANTS ARE HEAVY!
THEY ARE SPECIAL PLANTS BUTTERFLIES LOVE... LIKE CONEFLOWERS AND BEE BALM!
HUFF! HUFF!
♫ WHISTLE WHILE YOU WORK... ♫
MISS MALONE, WHEN DO WE GET TO RELEASE THE BUTTERFLIES?
ANY DAY NOW.
AS SOON AS THEY EMERGE FROM THEIR CHRYSALIS, WE'LL SET THEM FREE UP ON OUR ROOF.
I HOPE THEY'LL LAY THEIR EGGS HERE IN THEIR NEW HOME!
"MEANWHILE IN MISS MALONE'S BUTTERFLY LAB...
WELL, HELLO, MR. MONARCH. YOU WOULDN'T HAPPEN TO KNOW WHERE I COULD FIND OUR BUDDY, ALBERT? SIGH HE PROBABLY THOUGHT I'D EAT HIM...

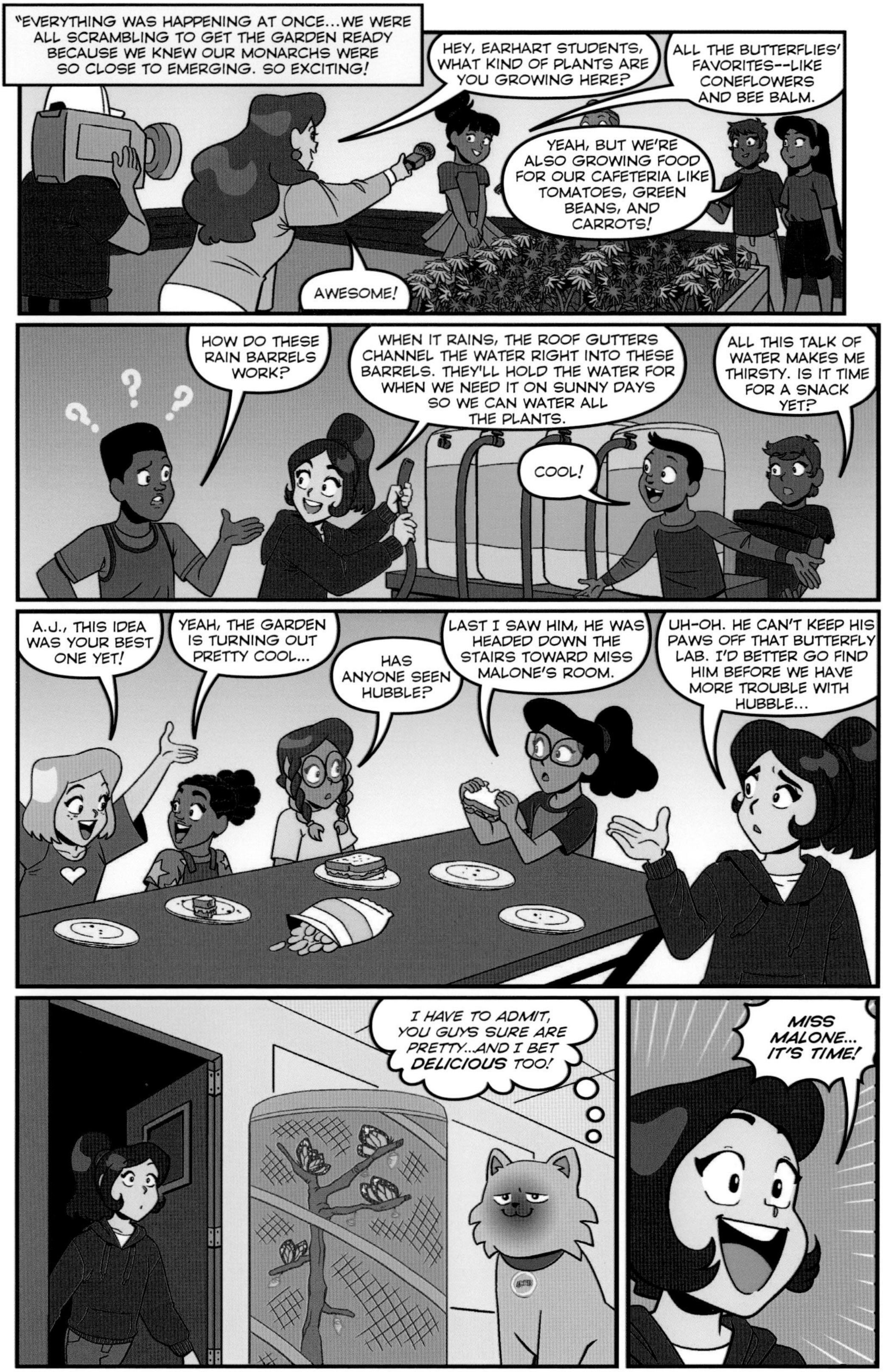
"EVERYTHING WAS HAPPENING AT ONCE...WE WERE ALL SCRAMBLING TO GET THE GARDEN READY BECAUSE WE KNEW OUR MONARCHS WERE SO CLOSE TO EMERGING. SO EXCITING!
HEY, EARHART STUDENTS, WHAT KIND OF PLANTS ARE YOU GROWING HERE?
ALL THE BUTTERFLIES' FAVORITES--LIKE CONEFLOWERS AND BEE BALM.
YEAH, BUT WE'RE ALSO GROWING FOOD FOR OUR CAFETERIA LIKE TOMATOES, GREEN BEANS, AND CARROTS!
AWESOME!
HOW DO THESE RAIN BARRELS WORK?
WHEN IT RAINS, THE ROOF GUTTERS CHANNEL THE WATER RIGHT INTO THESE BARRELS. THEY'LL HOLD THE WATER FOR WHEN WE NEED IT ON SUNNY DAYS SO WE CAN WATER ALL THE PLANTS.
COOL!
ALL THIS TALK OF WATER MAKES ME THIRSTY. IS IT TIME FOR A SNACK YET?
A.J., THIS IDEA WAS YOUR BEST ONE YET!
YEAH, THE GARDEN IS TURNING OUT PRETTY COOL...
HAS ANYONE SEEN HUBBLE?
LAST I SAW HIM, HE WAS HEADED DOWN THE STAIRS TOWARD MISS MALONE'S ROOM.
UH-OH. HE CAN'T KEEP HIS PAWS OFF THAT BUTTERFLY LAB. I'D BETTER GO FIND HIM BEFORE WE HAVE MORE TROUBLE WITH HUBBLE...
I HAVE TO ADMIT, YOU GUYS SURE ARE PRETTY...AND I BET DELICIOUS TOO!
MISS MALONE... IT'S TIME!

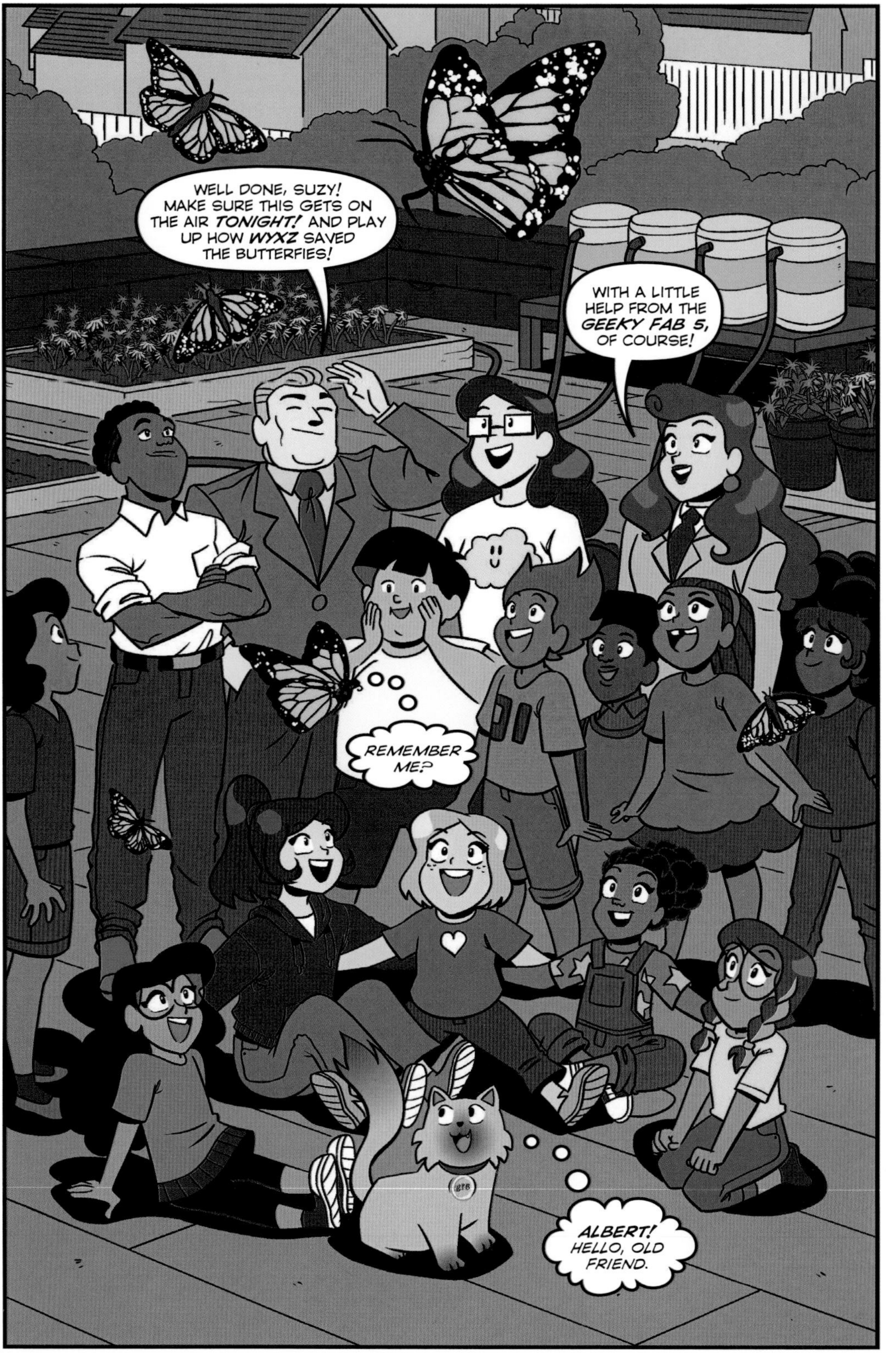
WELL DONE, SUZY! MAKE SURE THIS GETS ON THE AIR TONIGHT! AND PLAY UP HOW WYXZ SAVED THE BUTTERFIES!
WITH A LITTLE HELP FROM THE GEEKY FAB 5, OF COURSE!
REMEMBER ME?
ALBERT! HELLO, OLD FRIEND.

WATCH OUT FOR PAPERCUTZ

Welcome to the STEM-inspired, second GEEKY F@B #2 graphic novel, "The Mystery of the Missing Monarchs," by our favorite mother and daughter writing duo, Lucy & Liz Lareau, and drawn by Ryan Jampole & Jen Hernandez, all from Papercutz, the friendly butterfly-and-bee-loving folks dedicated to publishing great graphic novels for all ages. I'm Jim Salicrup, the Editor-in-Chief and Head Bee-Keeper, here to offer a little behind-the-scenes info...

While it can sometimes seem like everyone in the world has gone crazy and is doing all sorts of things that don't make any sense, the important thing is for you to never give up hope. *SPOILER ALERT* Just as it seemed that there was no way the Geeky F@b 5 could save their secret magical garden, a creative solution was found. While it would've been easy at several points for Lucy, A.J., Sofia, Zara, and Marina to give up, and possibly even become bitter about what was happening, they kept trying to find a way to solve their problem. In real life, we face problems every day. We may not be lucky enough to solve every problem, but we must always keep trying. Sometimes, like in "The Mystery of the Missing Monarchs," the answer can literally be right under your nose! The trick is to be able to allow yourself to be open to all possibilities, and not to get stuck on only one possible solution.

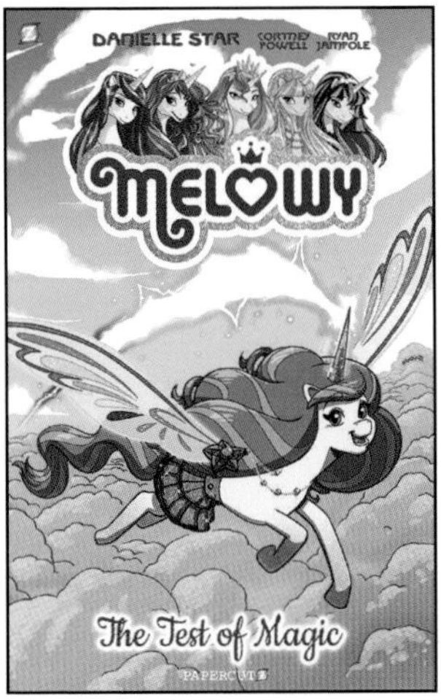
DANIELLE STAR
CORTNEY POWELL
RYAN JAMPOLE
MELOWY
The Test of Magic
PAPERCUTZ

Speaking of solving problems, let's give a great big THANK YOU to Jen Hernandez, who came aboard when we realized that we had overbooked Ryan Jampole. Not only was Ryan scheduled to draw THE GEEKY F@B 5, but he's also the artist of the all-new, fun fantasy series from Papercutz called MELOWY. So Ryan was scheduled to go from drawing Lucy, A.J., Sofia, Zara, and Marina—THE GEEKY F@B 5—to illustrating the latest adventure of Cleo, Electra, Maya, Cora, and Selina—the five flying unicorn stars of MELOWY—but we didn't allow enough time for Ryan to do his usual great job on both titles. Something had to be done. In this case, Jen was able to leap in and finish up a whole bunch of GEEKY F@B 5 pages working just from Ryan's layouts. We think she did a wonderful job! Likewise, when colorist Matt Herms ran into a scheduling conflict, we were super-lucky to get Laurie E. Smith to seamlessly complete the coloring. THANK YOU, Laurie! And an extra special THANK YOU to Wilson Ramos Jr., who was inadvertently given an earlier draft of the script, and was able to re-do his lettering in record time. While this may not seem to be as important as helping to save an endangered species, who knows? What if this graphic novel inspires you to do exactly that?

For those of you paying super-close attention, you probably noticed that I mentioned that Ryan Jampole's other assignment at Papercutz is illustrating a graphic novel series about flying unicorns. Yes, it's true. That series is called MELOWY, and when I first told Lucy Lareau about MELOWY she asked if the Melowies pooped rainbows! I said, no, but the Dreamworks TROLLS, stars of another Papercutz graphic novel series do poot cupcakes! To satisfy your curiosity about MELOWY, we're presenting a short preview of MELOWY #1 "The Test of Magic," by Danielle Star, creator; Cortney Powell, writer; Ryan Jampole, artist; Laurie E. Smith, colorist; and Wilson Ramos Jr., letterer on the following pages. Somehow it seems fitting to go from science-based comics to fantasy-filled comics, no?

In case you're wondering why Lucy isn't co-writing this Watch Out for Papercutz page like she did in GEEKY F@B 5 #1, the answer is that she's hard at work writing GEEKY F@B 5 #3 "Doggone Catstrophe" with her mom, that'll be coming your way soon via your favorite bookseller or library. We'll see you again then, but in the meantime, here's an awesome pic of Lucy with her BFFs, GEEKY F@B 5 and Hubble we thought you'd enjoy...

Thanks, Jim

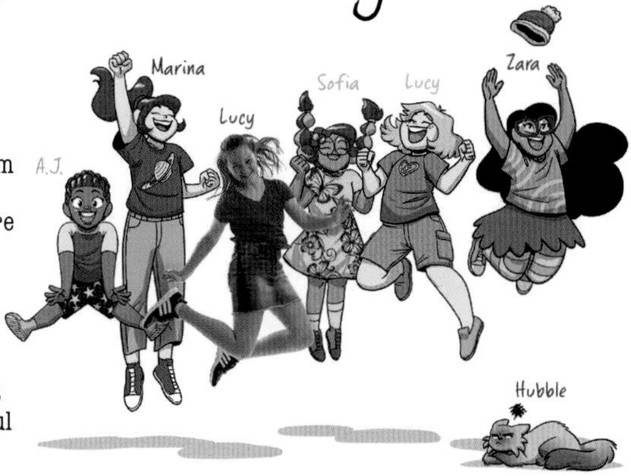
Marina
Sofia
Lucy
Zara
Lucy
A.J.
Hubble

STAY IN TOUCH!

EMAIL:	salicrup@papercutz.com
WEB:	papercutz.com
TWITTER:	@papercutzgn
INSTAGRAM:	@papercutzgn
FACEBOOK:	PAPERCUTZGRAPHICNOVELS
FAN MAIL:	Papercutz, 160 Broadway, Suite 700, East Wing, New York, NY 10038

Special preview of MELOWY #1

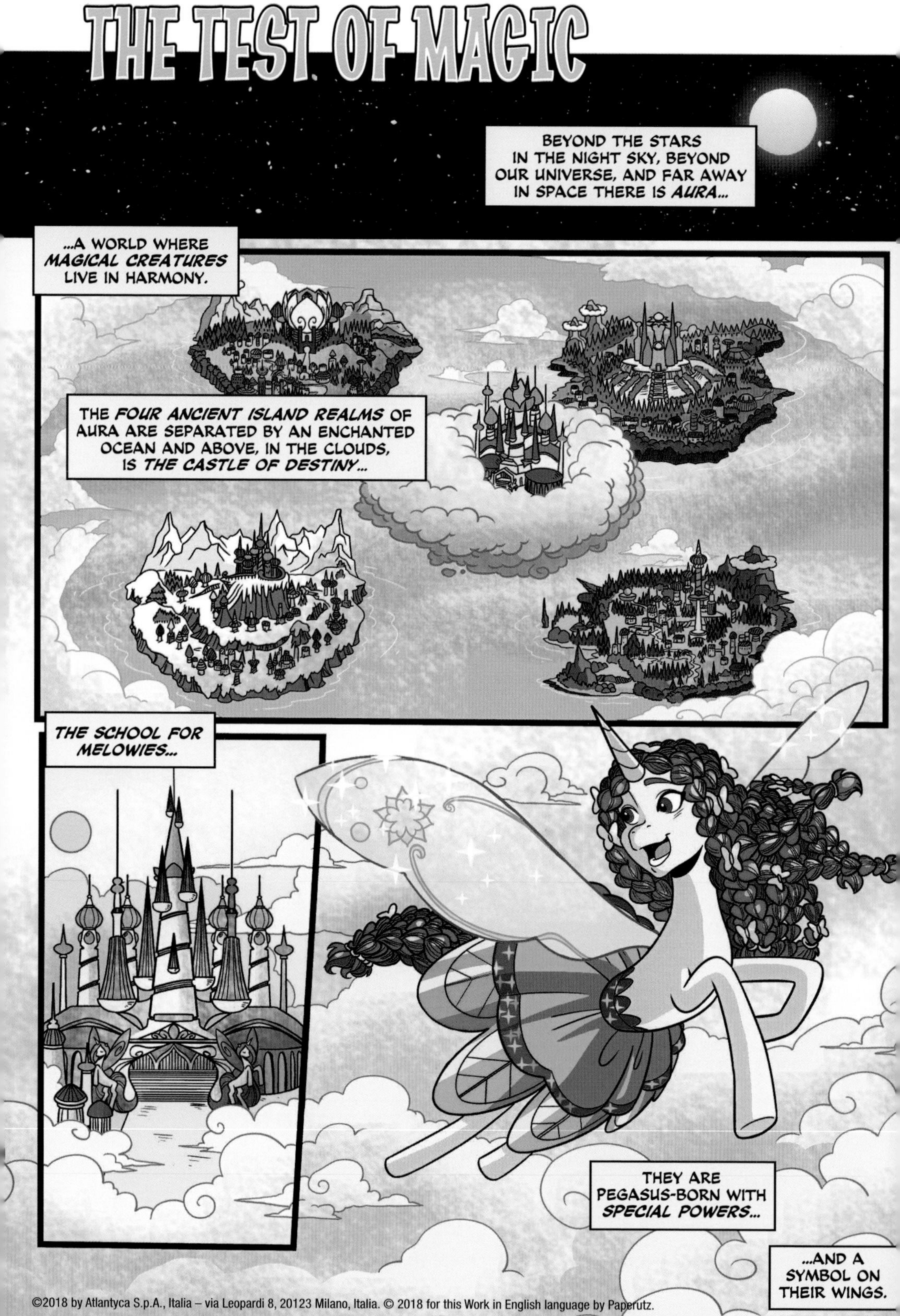
THE TEST OF MAGIC
BEYOND THE STARS IN THE NIGHT SKY, BEYOND OUR UNIVERSE, AND FAR AWAY IN SPACE THERE IS AURA...
...A WORLD WHERE MAGICAL CREATURES LIVE IN HARMONY.
THE FOUR ANCIENT ISLAND REALMS OF AURA ARE SEPARATED BY AN ENCHANTED OCEAN AND ABOVE, IN THE CLOUDS, IS THE CASTLE OF DESTINY...
THE SCHOOL FOR MELOWIES...
THEY ARE PEGASUS-BORN WITH SPECIAL POWERS...
...AND A SYMBOL ON THEIR WINGS.

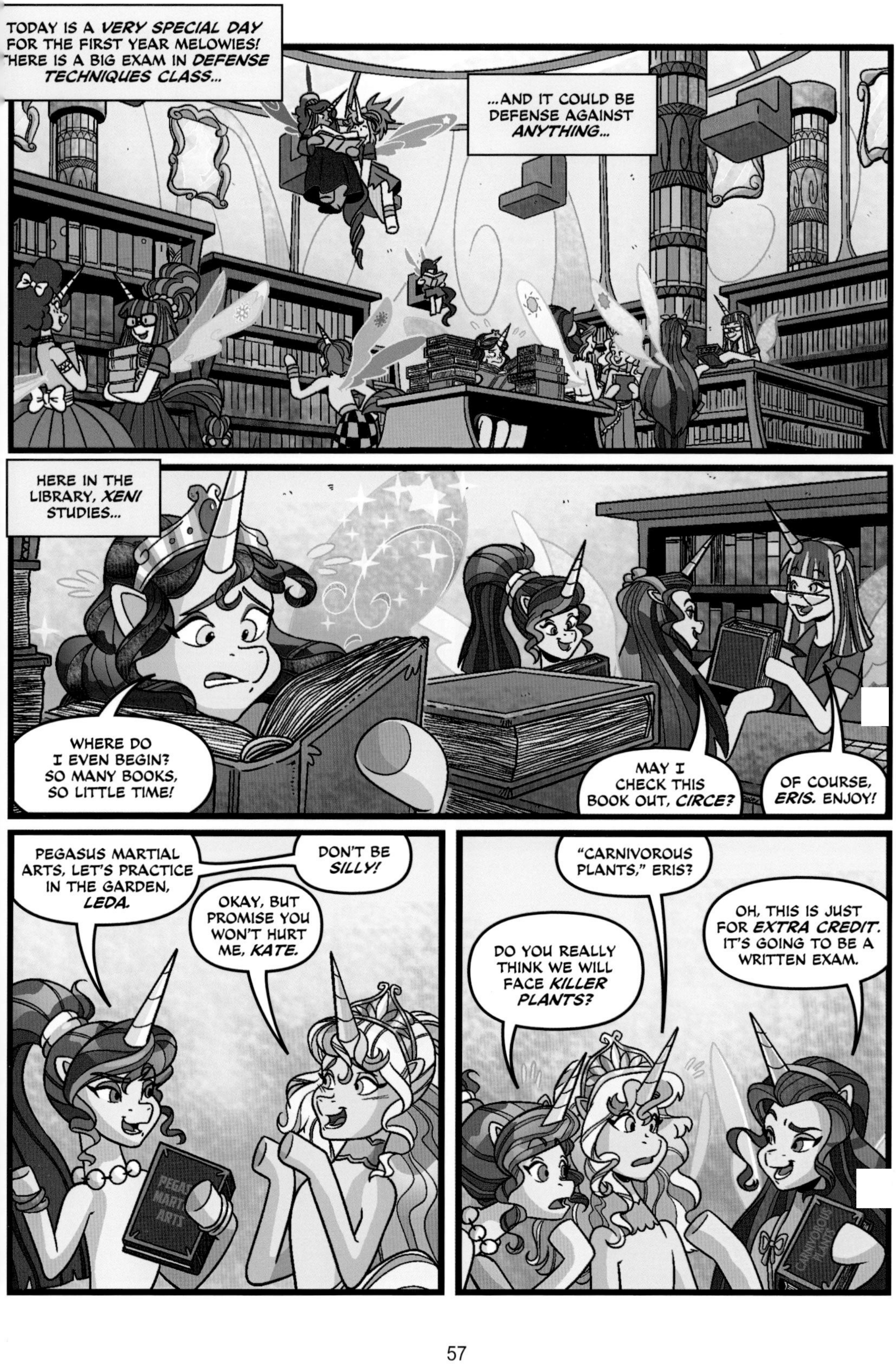
TODAY IS A *VERY SPECIAL DAY* FOR THE FIRST YEAR MELOWIES! THERE IS A BIG EXAM IN *DEFENSE TECHNIQUES CLASS*...
...AND IT COULD BE DEFENSE AGAINST *ANYTHING*...
HERE IN THE LIBRARY, *XENI* STUDIES...
WHERE DO I EVEN BEGIN? SO MANY BOOKS, SO LITTLE TIME!
MAY I CHECK THIS BOOK OUT, *CIRCE?*
OF COURSE, *ERIS.* ENJOY!
PEGASUS MARTIAL ARTS, LET'S PRACTICE IN THE GARDEN, *LEDA.*
OKAY, BUT PROMISE YOU WON'T HURT ME, *KATE.*
DON'T BE *SILLY!*
"CARNIVOROUS PLANTS," ERIS?
DO YOU REALLY THINK WE WILL FACE *KILLER PLANTS?*
OH, THIS IS JUST FOR *EXTRA CREDIT.* IT'S GOING TO BE A WRITTEN EXAM.
CARNIVOROUS PLANTS

MEANWHILE, IN THEIR DORM ROOM, FIVE MELOWIES ARE STUDYING TOGETHER, AS THESE FIVE DO *EVERYTHING* TOGETHER...

JUST FINISHED A BOOK ON *PEGASUS WARRIORS*, IT'S SO FASCINATING.

COULD YOU PASS THE *ORGANIC POTIONS* BOOK, *CLEO*?

HOW DO YOU READ SO FAST, CLEO?

WE ALL HAVE OUR TALENTS. *MAYA*, HOW DO YOU BAKE THE MOST DELICIOUS *HONEY BLUEBERRY SCONES*?

IT'S EASY! YOU JUST TAKE RIPE BLUEBERRIES WITH SOME RAW HONEY, BUTTER, CREAM--

BUT *THAT* ISN'T GOING TO HELP ME PASS THIS EXAM!

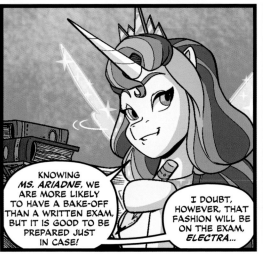

KNOWING *MS. ARIADNE*, WE ARE MORE LIKELY TO HAVE A BAKE-OFF THAN A WRITTEN EXAM, BUT IT IS GOOD TO BE PREPARED JUST IN CASE!

I DOUBT, HOWEVER, THAT FASHION WILL BE ON THE EXAM, *ELECTRA*...

MAYBE NOT, *CORA*, BUT IT JUST SO HAPPENS THAT THIS PARTICULAR FASHION QUEEN I'M READING ABOUT WAS ALSO A *WARRIOR*.

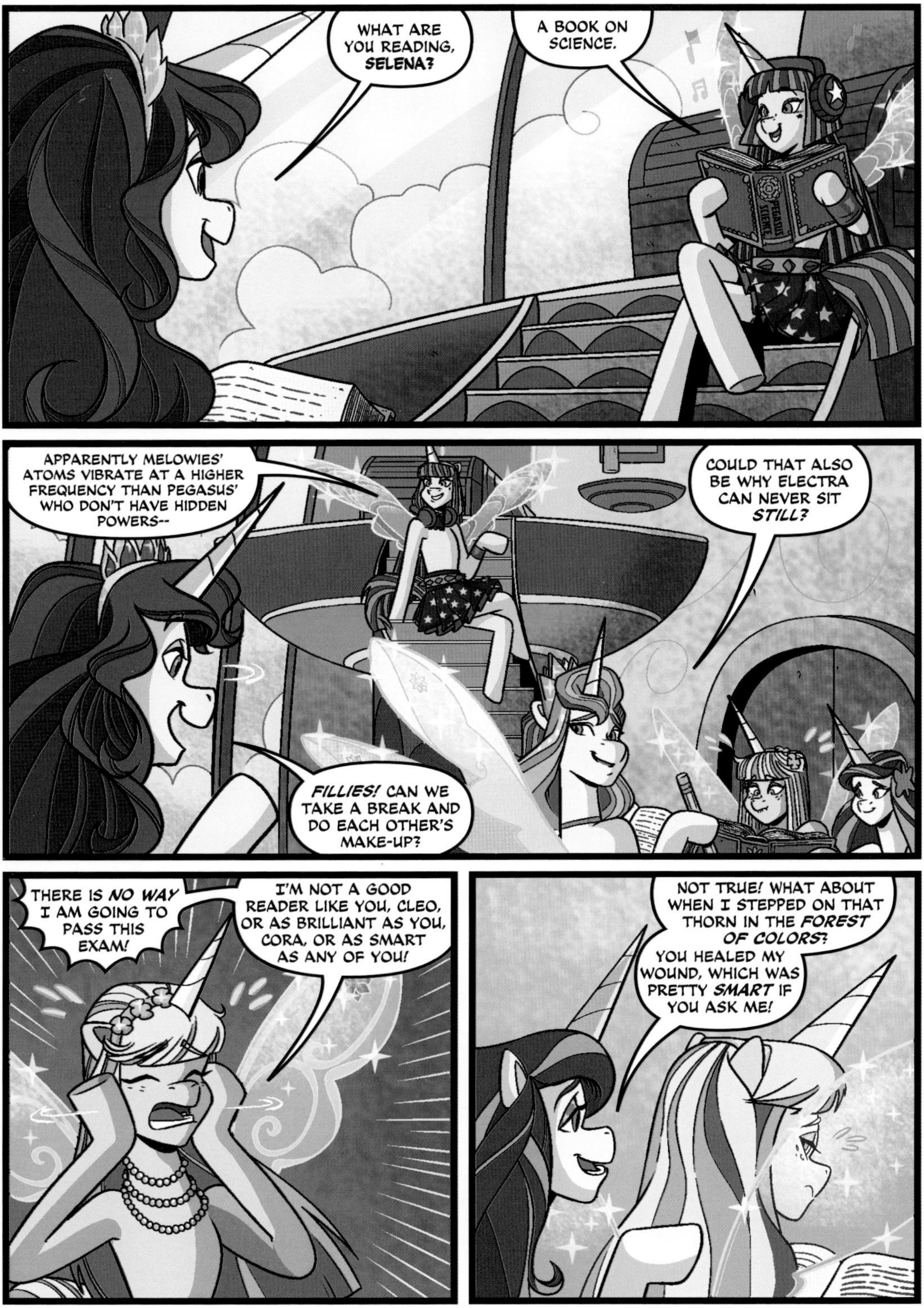
WHAT ARE YOU READING, SELENA?
A BOOK ON SCIENCE.
PEGASUS SCIENCE
APPARENTLY MELOWIES' ATOMS VIBRATE AT A HIGHER FREQUENCY THAN PEGASUS' WHO DON'T HAVE HIDDEN POWERS--
COULD THAT ALSO BE WHY ELECTRA CAN NEVER SIT STILL?
FILLIES! CAN WE TAKE A BREAK AND DO EACH OTHER'S MAKE-UP?
THERE IS NO WAY I AM GOING TO PASS THIS EXAM!
I'M NOT A GOOD READER LIKE YOU, CLEO, OR AS BRILLIANT AS YOU, CORA, OR AS SMART AS ANY OF YOU!
NOT TRUE! WHAT ABOUT WHEN I STEPPED ON THAT THORN IN THE FOREST OF COLORS?
YOU HEALED MY WOUND, WHICH WAS PRETTY SMART IF YOU ASK ME!

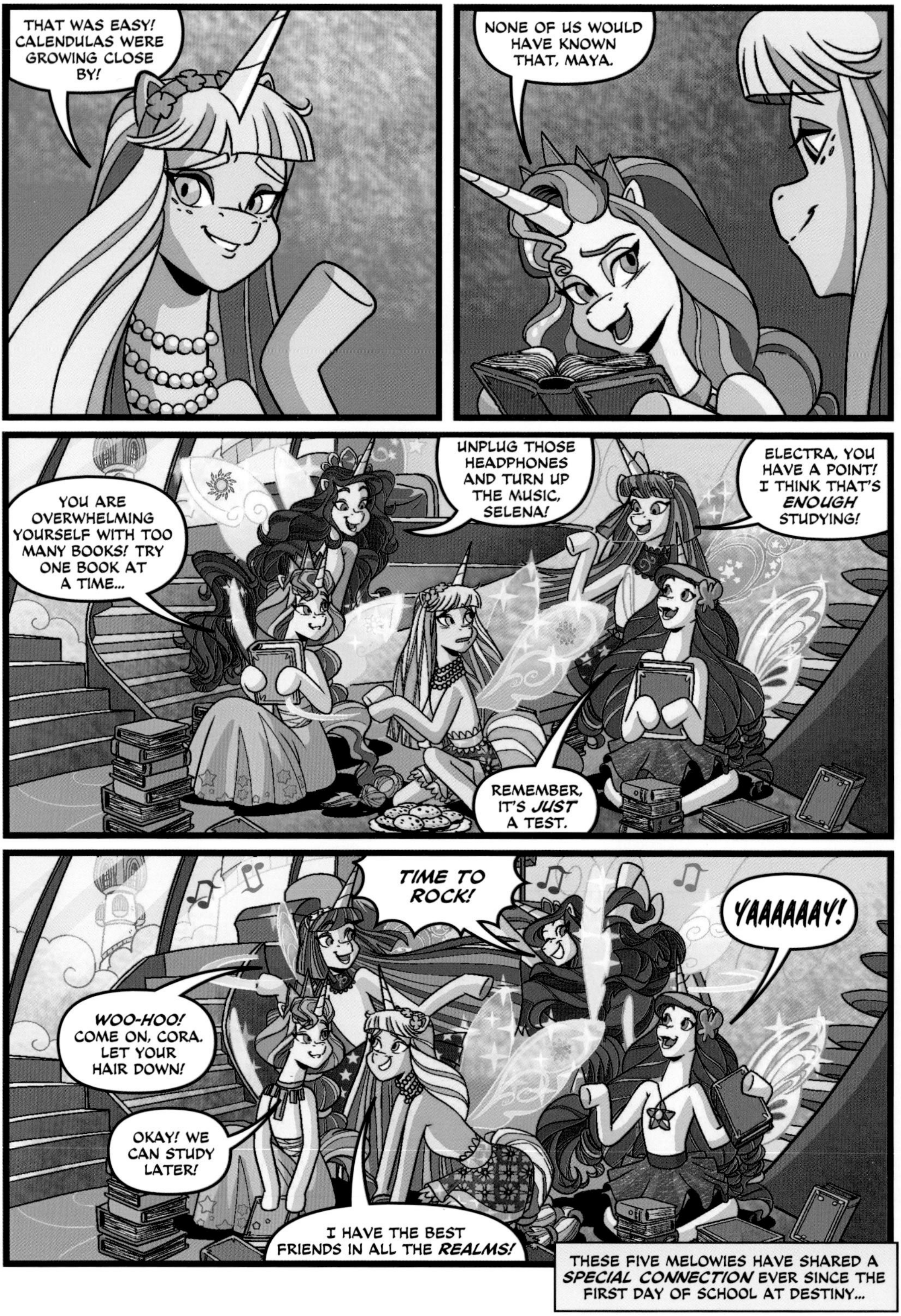
THAT WAS EASY! CALENDULAS WERE GROWING CLOSE BY!
NONE OF US WOULD HAVE KNOWN THAT, MAYA.
YOU ARE OVERWHELMING YOURSELF WITH TOO MANY BOOKS! TRY ONE BOOK AT A TIME...
UNPLUG THOSE HEADPHONES AND TURN UP THE MUSIC, SELENA!
ELECTRA, YOU HAVE A POINT! I THINK THAT'S *ENOUGH* STUDYING!
REMEMBER, IT'S *JUST* A TEST.
TIME TO ROCK!
YAAAAAAY!
WOO-HOO! COME ON, CORA. LET YOUR HAIR DOWN!
OKAY! WE CAN STUDY LATER!
I HAVE THE BEST FRIENDS IN ALL THE *REALMS!*
THESE FIVE MELOWIES HAVE SHARED A *SPECIAL CONNECTION* EVER SINCE THE FIRST DAY OF SCHOOL AT DESTINY...

THEY EACH FLEW UP FROM A DIFFERENT *REALM*...

...EAGER TO START LEARNING ABOUT THEIR *HIDDEN POWERS.*

CORA FLEW UP FROM THE *WINTER REALM,* WITH THE INTENT TO BE THE BEST, BUT NEVER EXPECTING TO FIND NEW BEST FRIENDS...

ELECTRA FLEW UP FROM THE *DAY REALM,* ALONG WITH HER BUBBLY PERSONALITY TO SPREAD HUMOR AND CHEER...

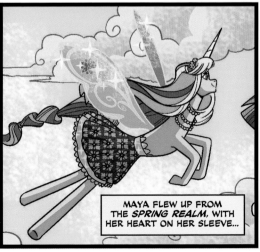

MAYA FLEW UP FROM THE *SPRING REALM,* WITH HER HEART ON HER SLEEVE...

AND SELENA FLEW UP FROM THE *NIGHT REALM,* WITH HER HEART HIDDEN BEHIND HER ALOOF FACADE.

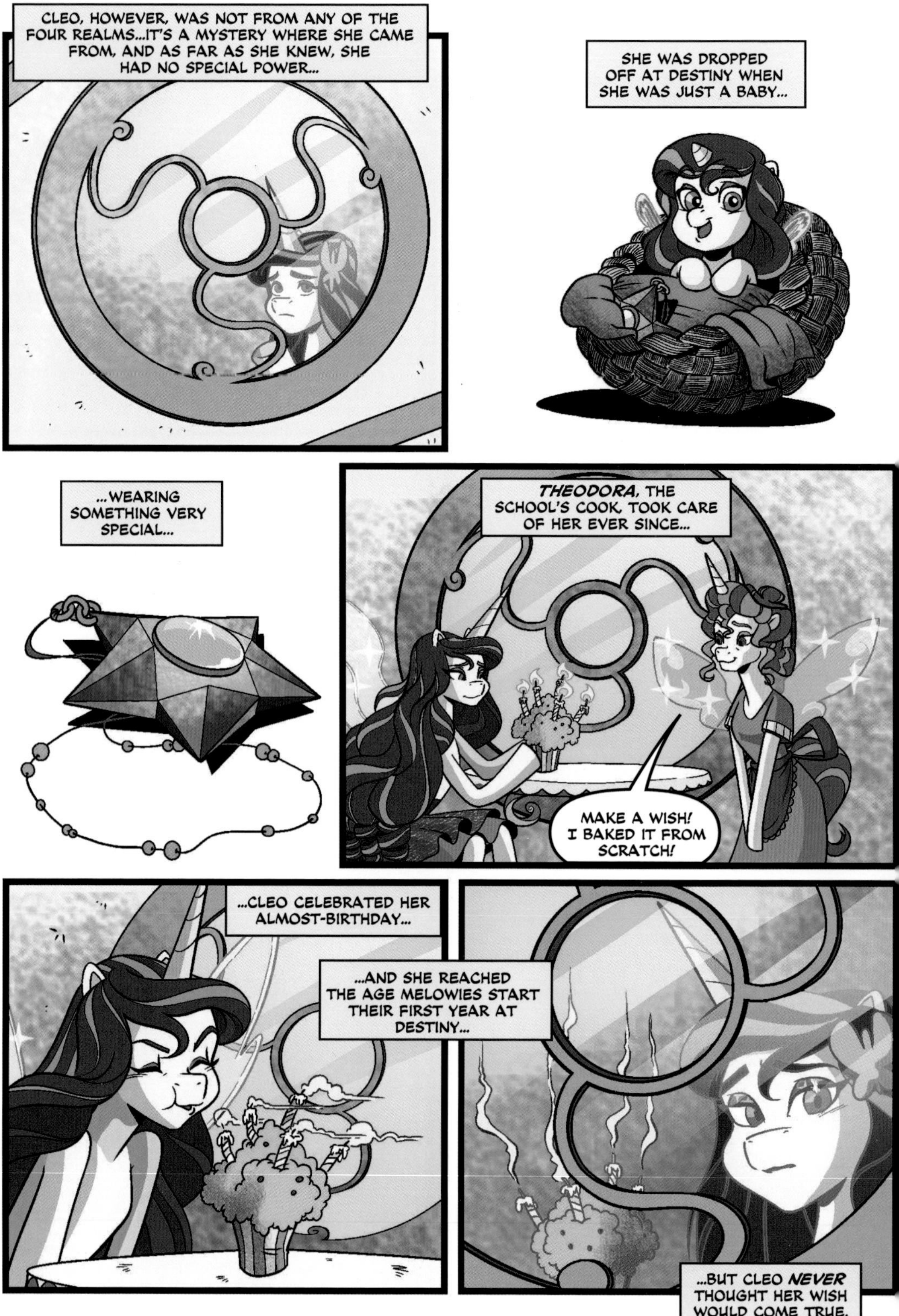
CLEO, HOWEVER, WAS NOT FROM ANY OF THE FOUR REALMS...IT'S A MYSTERY WHERE SHE CAME FROM, AND AS FAR AS SHE KNEW, SHE HAD NO SPECIAL POWER...
SHE WAS DROPPED OFF AT DESTINY WHEN SHE WAS JUST A BABY...
...WEARING SOMETHING VERY SPECIAL...
THEODORA, THE SCHOOL'S COOK, TOOK CARE OF HER EVER SINCE...
MAKE A WISH! I BAKED IT FROM SCRATCH!
...CLEO CELEBRATED HER ALMOST-BIRTHDAY...
...AND SHE REACHED THE AGE MELOWIES START THEIR FIRST YEAR AT DESTINY...
...BUT CLEO NEVER THOUGHT HER WISH WOULD COME TRUE.

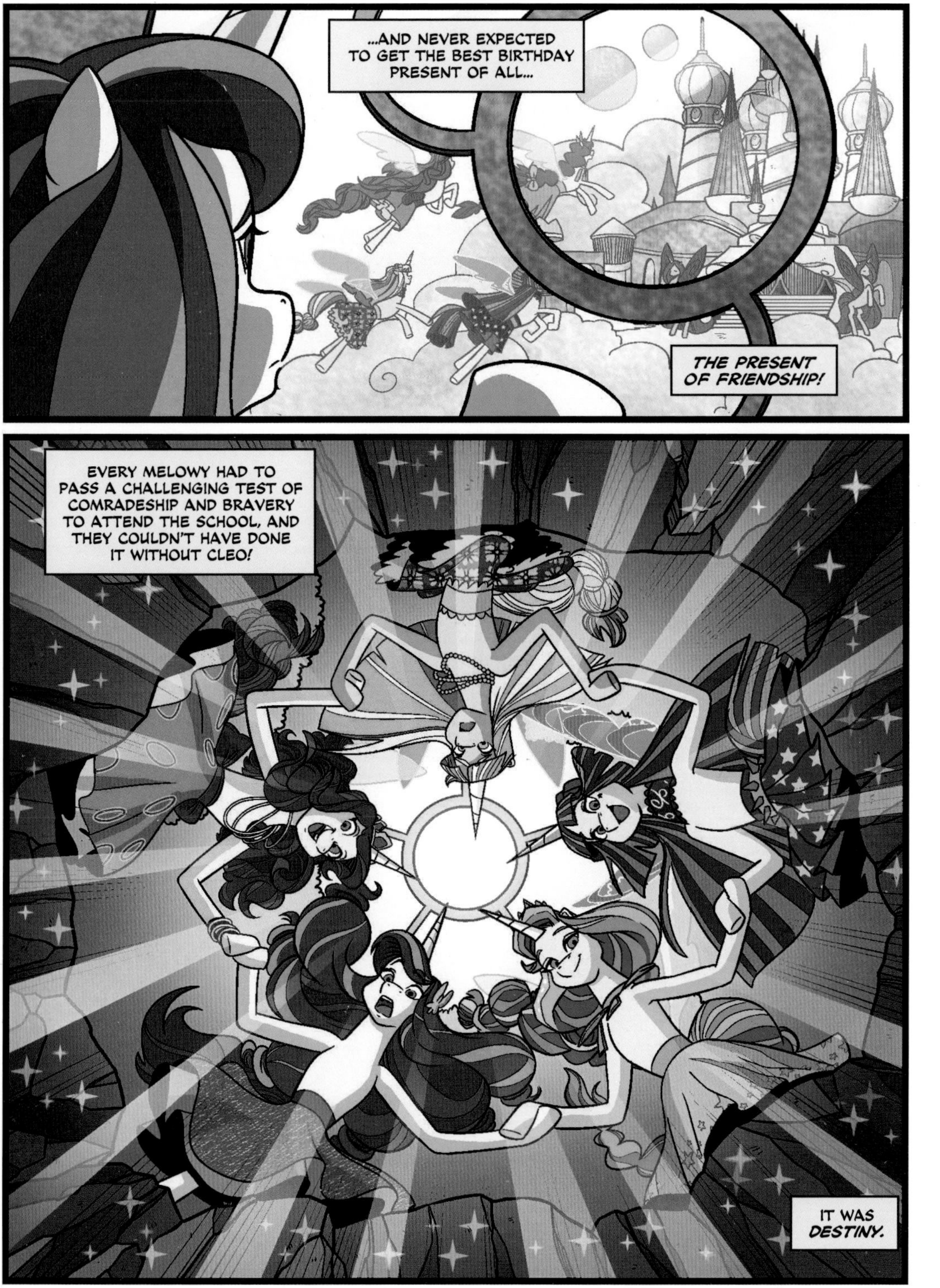
...AND NEVER EXPECTED TO GET THE BEST BIRTHDAY PRESENT OF ALL...
THE PRESENT OF FRIENDSHIP!
EVERY MELOWY HAD TO PASS A CHALLENGING TEST OF COMRADESHIP AND BRAVERY TO ATTEND THE SCHOOL, AND THEY COULDN'T HAVE DONE IT WITHOUT CLEO!
IT WAS DESTINY.

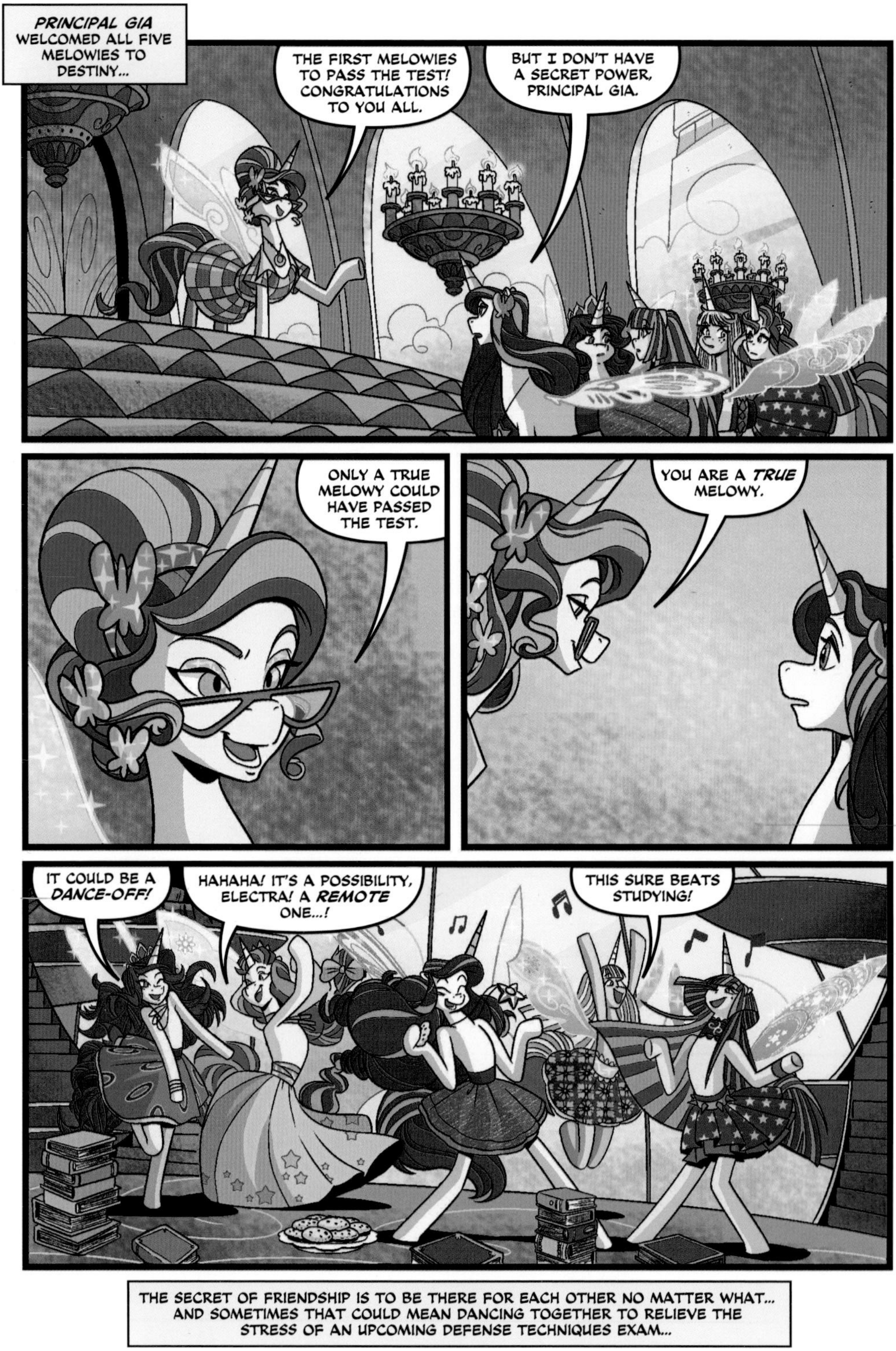
PRINCIPAL GIA WELCOMED ALL FIVE MELOWIES TO DESTINY...
THE FIRST MELOWIES TO PASS THE TEST! CONGRATULATIONS TO YOU ALL.
BUT I DON'T HAVE A SECRET POWER, PRINCIPAL GIA.
ONLY A TRUE MELOWY COULD HAVE PASSED THE TEST.
YOU ARE A TRUE MELOWY.
IT COULD BE A DANCE-OFF!
HAHAHA! IT'S A POSSIBILITY, ELECTRA! A REMOTE ONE...!
THIS SURE BEATS STUDYING!
THE SECRET OF FRIENDSHIP IS TO BE THERE FOR EACH OTHER NO MATTER WHAT... AND SOMETIMES THAT COULD MEAN DANCING TOGETHER TO RELIEVE THE STRESS OF AN UPCOMING DEFENSE TECHNIQUES EXAM...

See what happens in next in MELOWY #1 "The Test of Magic," available at booksellers and libraries everywhere.

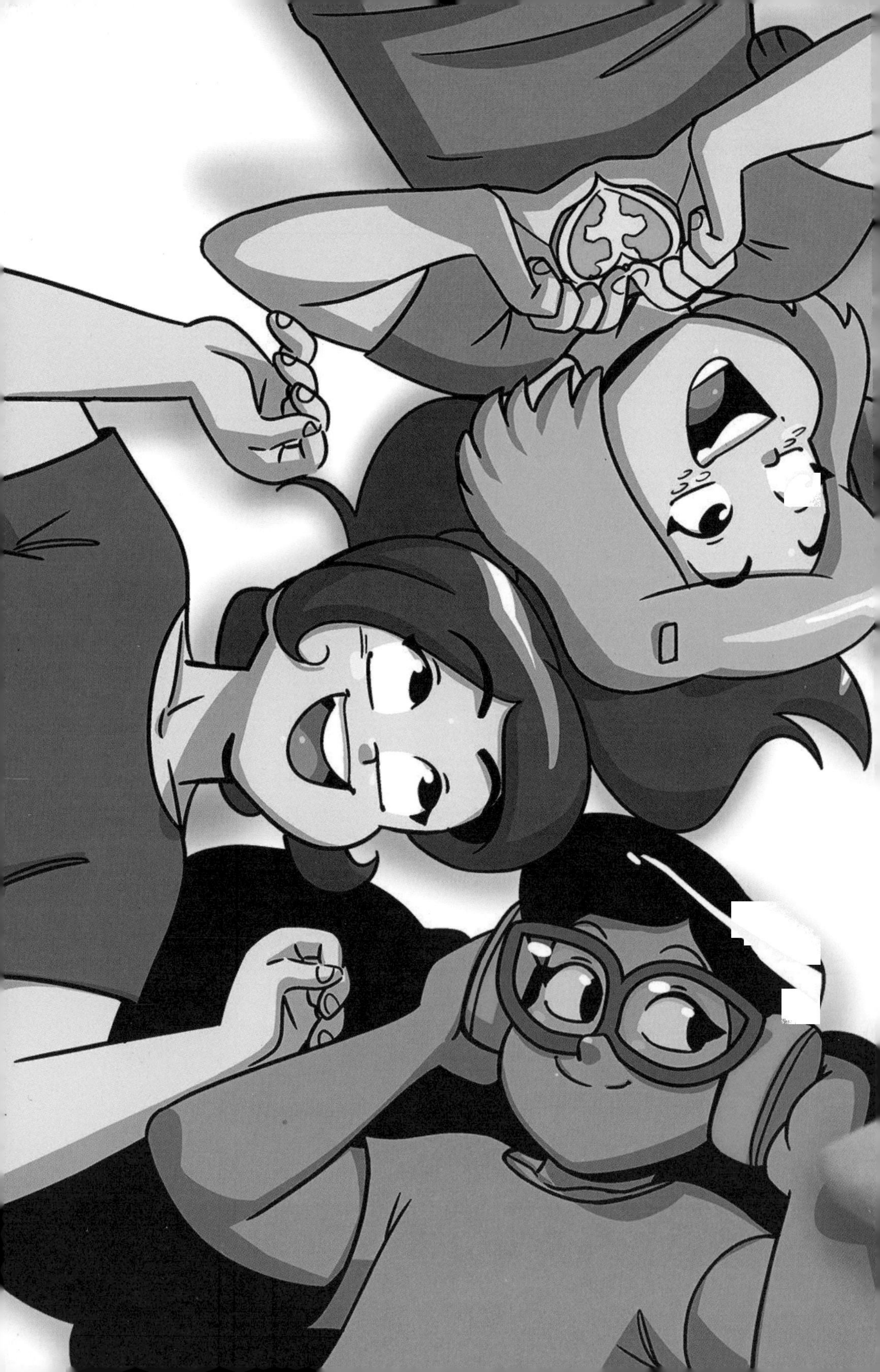